Kristy and the Vampires

Kristy and the Vampires
Ann M. Martin

AN
APPLE
PAPERBACK

SCHOLASTIC INC.
New York Toronto London Auckland Sydney

*The author gratefully acknowledges
Ellen Miles
for her help in
preparing this manuscript.*

ISBN 0-590-47053-1

Copyright © 1994 by Ann M. Martin. All rights reserved. Published
by Scholastic Inc. APPLE PAPERBACKS ® and THE BABY-SITTERS
CLUB ® are registered trademarks of Scholastic Inc.

12 11 10 9 8 7 6 5 4 3 2 1   4 5 6 7 8 9/9

Printed in the U.S.A.   40

First Scholastic printing, June 1994

CHAPTER 1

I'll probably always remember that Wednesday as The Day I Found Out It Was Going to Be an Interesting Summer. It was a hot day — a *very* hot day, with no breeze and a sky that looked almost white. I was baby-sitting for David Michael and Emily Michelle, my little brother and sister, and the three of us were sitting on the front stoop eating sandwiches.

"It's *hot*," complained David Michael, wiping his forehead with a jelly-smeared hand.

"Hot!" repeated a pink-cheeked Emily Michelle, who was sitting between David Michael and me.

"I know." I sighed. "It sure is." Summer vacation had only started a couple of weeks ago, and already I was starting to think school wasn't such a bad thing. I mean, it's nice to have a break from classes, but sometimes summer vacation can seem awfully long and boring. Long and boring and *hot*.

My name's Kristy Thomas, or if you want to be formal, Kristin Amanda Thomas. I'm thirteen, and I go to Stoneybrook Middle School, which is in Stoneybrook, Connecticut. I've lived all my life in Stoneybrook, and it's a nice little town. But guess what? It can be boring.

Oh, I keep pretty busy. I'm president of this terrific club, for one thing. It's called the BSC, for Baby-sitters Club, and it's really more like a business than a club. But more about that later. I also coach a softball team, Kristy's Krushers, for kids who are too young or otherwise not ready for Little League. And I also stay busy baby-sitting for my younger brothers and sisters and keeping track of the rest of my family, which is pretty humongous and complicated.

I have two older brothers, Sam and Charlie. Sam's fifteen, and Charlie's seventeen, and they're okay as far as big brothers go. They're both involved in their own things, mostly school activities. Otherwise, Charlie mainly works on his car, which we call the Junk Bucket (it's not exactly new, as you might've guessed), and as for Sam, well, he's mostly interested in girls.

David Michael, my younger brother, is seven and a half. He has dark hair, like the rest of my family, but *his* hair has these soft little curls that are the envy of all my friends. David Michael is a great kid: he's serious and deliberate and he's a little klutzy at sports, but he's also very loving and has a terrific sense of humor.

When David Michael was just a baby, my father walked out on our family. I remember my dad, but not all that well. He was never very involved as a parent, and I guess that's partly why he left — he just wasn't interested in being a daddy. He hardly stays in touch with us at all. In fact, I'm not even sure exactly where he is. Last I heard, he was in California, but for all I know he could be in Alaska or Japan by now.

I don't think my mom has ever forgiven my father for what he did, but she never sat around whining about how badly he treated us. My mom is a very strong woman, and when my dad left she knew she wouldn't have any spare time to spend complaining. Instead, she worked hard to raise my brothers and me by herself, and I've always admired her for doing it as well as she did.

After years of being a single mother, my mom finally got a good break. She met and fell in love with a really nice guy named Watson Brewer, who happens to be mega-rich.

Watson is now my stepfather, and while I wasn't totally crazy about him at first, he's really grown on me.

Now Mom still works, and my brothers and I live in his huge house (it's more like a mansion, really), which is way across town from where I used to live. Our family has grown, too. I now have a sweet little stepbrother named Andrew, who's four, and a seven-year-old stepsister named Karen. She's a real bundle of energy. Karen and Andrew live with us every other month now. (It's a new arrangement.)

My other new sibling is Emily Michelle, who's two and a half. Mom and Watson adopted her not that long ago. Emily, who's Vietnamese, is awfully cute, with her shiny black hair in bangs across her forehead and her pudgy cheeks. She's had a hard time learning to speak English, but she's coming along with it lately.

After Mom and Watson adopted Emily, my grandmother Nannie came to live with us, too, just to help out. Nannie probably has more energy than the rest of us put together; she never sits still. She has this great old car we call the Pink Clinker, and she's always taking off in it. She goes bowling, to aqua-aerobics classes, poker tournaments — you name it, she does it.

So that's my family! Oh, I almost forgot to mention the non-human members of the Thomas-Brewer clan: we have a Bernese Mountain dog puppy named Shannon, and a cranky old cat named Boo-Boo. Plus, Karen and Andrew have a rat and a hermit crab, which travel back and forth with them, and a couple of goldfish.

Anyway, you can see how my family and my other activities might keep me busy. But somehow, on that hot summer Wednesday, I was worried that I wasn't going to be busy *enough*.

"I'm *bored*," said David Michael, popping the last bite of his sandwich into his mouth. "Let's *do* something."

"Sure," I said. "What do you feel like doing?"

"I don't know." He sighed, leaning back. "Just *something*."

"Play Candyland?" asked Emily Michelle hopefully. She loves that game, but none of the rest of us can stand it.

"No way, José," said David Michael. He spotted yesterday's paper, which I had brought outside. "Read us the funnies, Kristy," he said, picking it up and giving it to me. "You always do the voices so good."

"So *well*," I said, correcting him automatically as I took the paper. I turned to the funny pages and glanced through the comics. None of them seemed especially hilarious, but I started to read aloud anyway. "What are you doing, Sarge?" I began, showing David Michael and Emily the page so they could see Beetle Bailey. I went through that one and three others, and then I started to lose interest. I usually love the comics, but on a hot summer day, even they can be dull. My eyes wandered over the page until suddenly something in the "Around Stoneybrook" column, which is always at the top of the comics section, caught my eye.

"What's this?" I said. " 'Stoneybrookites are in for some excitement this summer,' " I read out loud, " 'as Hollywood comes to Connecticut. It's all very hush-hush so far, but keep your eyes and ears out for that Lights, Camera, Action.' Hmmm. Wonder what *that's* all about."

"They're making a movie here," said David Michael, as if it were old news. "Didn't you hear about it?"

"No!" I said. "How do *you* know about it?"

"Linny told me," David Michael said. Linny Papadakis is a neighborhood boy who's a good friend of David Michael's. "His dad knows all about it. He heard about it down at the hardware store."

A movie! Now *that* sounded interesting.

"When are they going to start? Who's in it? What's it about?" I was dying to know more.

David Michael shrugged. "It's just a movie," he said. "That's all I know." He didn't seem too excited — in fact, he seemed as bored as ever.

"Read more!" cried Emily Michelle just then, pointing to the funny pages. I noticed that her hands, like David Michael's, were covered with jelly.

"Okay," I said, "but first it's time to get you cleaned up." I herded her and David Michael into the kitchen and helped them wash their hands. Then I spent a little time cleaning up the mess we'd made putting together our sandwiches. As I wiped down the counter, I wondered about the movie. Would there be any big stars in it? Why were they making a movie in *Stoneybrook*? Would they be hiring any locals to work as extras? The idea of a movie crew coming to my little town suddenly made the summer seem a lot more promising.

By the time I finished cleaning up, Emily Michelle was busy playing with her troll dolls and David Michael was involved in digging up a corner of the yard where he's convinced there's buried treasure. He digs there every once in a while, but so far he hasn't found a thing.

I sat on the porch steps, watching them both

and trying to figure out how I could learn more about the movie. I was so deep in thought I didn't even notice Mary Anne's arrival until Emily Michelle squealed "May-Anne!"

Mary Anne Spier, my best friend, is a big favorite of Emily Michelle's. Mary Anne and I are about as different as two people can be, but somehow it's never gotten in the way of our friendship. She's shy and very sensitive, while I'm like "a bull in a china shop," as Watson would say. That means I kind of charge into things without thinking about the consequences. Mary Anne and I have always had *looks* in common — we're both short for our age and have brown hair and eyes — but recently Mary Anne has started to pay a little more attention than I do to clothes and haircuts and things. I hardly ever even look in the mirror, and I wear the same sorts of things every day: jeans (or shorts, when it's as hot as it was that day), running shoes, and a T-shirt.

Anyway, that afternoon Mary Anne had ridden up on her bicycle and hopped off before I even noticed. But as soon as Emily Michelle spotted her, I did, too. "Mary Anne!" I said. "Guess what?"

"Guess what?" she said at the same time, as she bent to hug Emily Michelle. "They're making a movie here!"

"That's what I just heard," I said. "Do you know anything about it?"

"Not much," she said. "Just that they're filming part of it at a house near mine."

"Really?" I asked. "How cool! We can go over and watch."

"And that it's a TV movie," Mary Anne continued, "and it's going to be called *Little Vampires*."

I grinned. *"Little Vampires?"* I repeated. That sounded like fun.

Mary Anne nodded. "It's about a group of boy vampires," she said. She looked thoughtful for a minute. "Do you think Cam Geary might be in it?" she asked hopefully.

Cam Geary is a TV star, and Mary Anne has had this major crush on him for what seems like forever. "Oh, Cam Geary," I said dismissively, rolling my eyes.

"Kristy!" said Mary Anne, looking hurt. "This might be my big chance to meet him!"

"Okay, okay," I said. "Maybe he'll be in it. Who knows? The important thing is, they're making a movie here. That means the summer can't possibly be as dull as I thought it was going to be."

Mary Anne and I hung out on the porch for awhile, speculating about the movie and playing trolls with Emily Michelle. About an hour later, Charlie turned up, and *he* started talking about the movie, too. The news was all over town, he said. He showed us an article in that afternoon's paper. "And I'm going to get a job on the crew," he announced importantly. "I'll be a gofer, an extra — anything. It says here they'll need local workers."

Charlie wasn't the only person who was excited about the movie. I definitely was, and I was sure all of my other friends would be, too. In fact, I knew right then that we'd be talking about nothing else that afternoon at our BSC meeting.

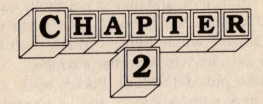

CHAPTER 2

As soon as our meeting crossed my mind, I realized Mary Anne and I were going to be late for it if we didn't start moving. Charlie was ready to go (he drives me to our meetings), so we threw Mary Anne's bicycle into the back of the Junk Bucket and took off, rattling and lurching down the street.

I checked my watch anxiously as we drove. If there's one thing I hate, it's being late for things. In fact, I always like to be a little early, *especially* for BSC meetings. I mean, I *am* the president, and it wouldn't be right for me to be late.

The whole idea for the BSC was mine, which is why I'm president. See, one day when my mom was trying to track down a sitter for David Michael, I realized that parents would love having one number they could call where they'd be sure to find a reliable sitter. So I got some friends together and we formed the BSC,

11

and it's been successful right from the start.

We meet three times a week, on Mondays, Wednesdays, and Fridays, from five-thirty until six. Parents can call during those times to set up sitting jobs, and they're practically guaranteed a sitter. Not to boast, since it *was* my idea, but the whole thing works so well we hardly ever have to advertise anymore.

Charlie pulled the Junk Bucket up to the curb, and with a cough and a sputter it stopped. He hopped out and lifted Mary Anne's bike onto the sidewalk. "See you soon, Nerd-Brain," he said to me.

"Later, Mush-Mouth," I answered.

"Thank you for the ride, Charlie," said Mary Anne politely, ignoring our rude exchange. She grew up as an only child, and she doesn't always understand brother-sister relationships. She parked her bike in the Kishis' driveway, and then she and I headed inside and up the stairs.

BSC meetings are always at the Kishi house, in Claudia's room, which is equipped with a handy private phone line. Claudia and Mary Anne and I have all known each other since we were in diapers (I used to live across the street from Claud, next door to Mary Anne's old house, before I moved to Watson's), so the Kishi house feels almost like home to me.

I checked my watch again as we ran up the stairs, and realized that it was only 5:20. "Whoops!" I muttered. That happens to me a lot: I rush so much to be on time that I end up arriving early.

But when we walked into Claud's room, it turned out that most of the other BSC members were already there. "Kristy!" said Jessi, who was sitting on the floor next to her best friend, Mal. "Guess what! They're going to be making a — "

"Movie!" I finished. "I heard. Isn't it awesome?" So *that* was why everybody had gotten there so early: to talk about the movie. "What do you all know about it?" I asked, settling into the director's chair by Claudia's desk, which is where I always sit.

"It's called *Baby Dracula*," said Claud, knowledgeably. She was sitting on her bed, trying to open a bag of Oreos with her teeth. "My dad heard about it from the plumber."

Mary Anne cracked up. "*Little Vampires*," she corrected. She had sat down next to Claud, and was checking out the club record book. As our secretary, she's responsible for keeping it up-to-date.

"Right," said Claud agreeably, popping an Oreo into her mouth and offering the bag around.

"I heard it was going to have all these big stars in it!" said Shannon, helping herself to a couple of cookies.

Mary Anne started to get that Cam Geary look in her eyes again, but before she could say anything, the phone rang. At the same time, Stacey walked in. Our meeting hadn't officially started yet, but now that Stacey had arrived, the entire BSC was on hand, so I answered the phone the way I do during meetings.

"Baby-sitters Club!" I said. "How can I help you?"

That one phone call explained a lot. By the time I hung up, I had learned much more about the movie. The call was from Mrs. Masters, the mother of two boys named Derek and Todd. Derek's eight, and Todd is four. Derek happens to be a big TV star, and the Masterses live in California while his show, *P.S. 162*, is being shot. But they have a house in Stoneybrook, too, which is why we count them as regular clients.

"Listen to this, guys," I said, as soon as I hung up. "Derek's in the movie! In fact, the whole reason the movie's being shot here is because the Masterses suggested Stoneybrook as the perfect small town setting."

"I knew it, I knew it, I knew it!" said Claud.

"You did?" asked Stacey, raising her eyebrows.

"Well, not really," Claudia admitted. "But I should have guessed."

"So what else did she say?" asked Mary Anne. I could tell she was dying to know whether Mrs. Masters had mentioned Cam Geary.

"Not much," I said, acting cool. "She just wondered if any of us might be interested in working on the set every day."

"WHAT?" everybody asked at once.

"There's supposed to be somebody on the set with Derek at all times," I explained calmly, even though I was just as excited as everyone else. "And Mr. and Mrs. Masters won't be able to be there every day. Plus, Todd has a small part, too, so they'll need somebody to watch him. Not every day, though."

"Me! Me! Me!" shouted Jessi, waving her hand as if she were in school.

"I'll do it!" said Stacey.

"Hold on, hold on," said Mary Anne, who was checking the record book. At a glance, she can tell which of us is available for a job, since she keeps track of all our schedules in the book. "I know we all think this job sounds great, but the fact is that most of us already have a lot of commitments for the summer.

We're *really* booked up for daytime work, since all the kids are out of school. In fact, the only person who could possibly take on the job with Derek is — " She flipped a couple of pages, and I could swear that every member of the BSC was holding her breath. "Kristy," she finished.

"Yess!" I said, throwing my fist into the air.

"And Claud could take the job with Todd," Mary Anne went on.

"All *right*!" said Claudia, through a mouthful of Oreos.

"The rest of us might be able to visit the set now and then, at least," said Mary Anne.

"Oh, I hope so," said Jessi. "I'd hate to miss the whole thing."

I called Mrs. Masters back to tell her the job was all set, trying to keep the call brief since it was long distance. We pay Claudia's phone bill with money from our treasury (we also pay Charlie to drive me to meetings), and I knew Stacey would get antsy if she saw me frittering away our precious dollars. As club treasurer, she collects dues (every Monday, without fail), and she keeps a tight hand on the money we accumulate.

Maybe I should stop here and explain a little about who the BSC members are and what they do, just to give you a more complete picture of the club.

As president, I run our meetings. I also work hard to keep generating new ideas for the club. For example, I came up with Kid-Kits, which are these boxes crammed full of hand-me-down toys and games, plus new stickers and crayons and things. The kids we sit for go wild when we bring them on jobs. I also thought of the club notebook, where we each write up all the jobs we go on. I have to admit, the notebook is not one of my most popular ideas. Most of the other club members aren't that crazy about writing in it, since it's a lot of work, but they do agree that it makes us better sitters, since we're all up-to-date on what's going on with our regular clients.

The member who likes the club notebook the least is probably Claudia, the BSC's vice president. She doesn't spell all that well, and I think she's sometimes embarrassed about her entries. Claud isn't dumb or anything, although she isn't a genius like her older sister Janine. It's just that Claudia doesn't "apply" herself, as her parents would say, to her schoolwork. What she *does* apply herself to is her artwork; Claud is the most creative and talented person I know. She also applies herself to eating as much junk food as possible, and to reading Nancy Drew books, two habits her parents aren't wild about.

Claudia is Japanese-American, and with her

long black hair, dark, almond-shaped eyes, and perfect complexion, she's beautiful. Her clothes look great, too, because she's as creative about dressing as she is about everything else. Claudia somehow knows how to put together a perfectly stunning outfit with odds and ends from a thrift store.

Claud is our vice-president mostly because of that private phone line in her room. She answers club calls when they come in at odd hours, but other than that, she doesn't really have many official duties.

Claud's best friend is Stacey McGill. The two of them share a passion for fashion: Stacey is about the trendiest dresser Stoneybrook has ever seen. She's from New York City, originally, and she still has that urban flair. Stacey has blonde hair, which is usually permed into a curly mass, and huge blue eyes. She's an only child. I think that made it doubly hard for her when her parents got divorced not that long ago. Her dad still lives in New York, and while Stacey chose to live with her mom in Stoneybrook, she makes a point of visiting her dad as often as possible.

Stacey does *not* share Claudia's passion for junk food — or at least, if she does, she manages to control it. She has to, since she's a diabetic. That means her body doesn't handle sugar well — in fact, she has to be extremely careful about keeping track of every single thing she eats. Not only that, she has to give herself shots of insulin every day! Stacey's what Watson would call "a trooper." She never complains about being diabetic — she just deals with it.

I'd have to say that Mary Anne is a kind of a trooper, too. She grew up without a mom, and that can't have been easy. Her mom died when Mary Anne was just a baby, which left Mary Anne's dad to bring her up all by himself. I remember years and years of him being extremely strict with her, but recently he's begun to treat her more like the responsible young adult she is.

There've been some other changes in her family, too. Mary Anne is no longer an only child. Now she has a stepbrother and a stepsister, and her stepsister happens to be her *other* best friend, Dawn Schafer. Dawn is a member of our club, too. But right now she's spending some time with her dad in California, where she grew up. Confusing, right? I'll try to explain. See, Dawn's mom was born and raised in Stoneybrook, but then moved to California, got married, and had two kids: Dawn and her younger brother Jeff. Then, when the Schafers divorced, Mrs. Schafer brought her kids back to Stoneybrook to live. Dawn and Mary Anne met, became friends, and discovered that their parents had dated when they were in high school. They got them back together, and the rest is history. Now the Spier-Schafer family (including Tigger, Mary Anne's kitten) lives happily together in the Schafers' cool old farmhouse.

Well, not the *whole* Spier-Schafer family. Even before Mrs. Schafer and Mr. Spier got married, Dawn's little brother decided he was miserable in Stoneybrook and ended up moving back to California. Dawn was okay with that, but after a while she missed Jeff and her dad so much that not long ago she went back, too, for an extended visit. Everybody in the BSC misses Dawn a ton, especially Mary Anne.

When Dawn's here with us, she serves as the club's alternate officer, which means she can fill in if one of the other officers can't make it to a meeting. For now, the job is being covered by Shannon Kilbourne, who is a friend of mine and lives in my new neighborhood. Shannon goes to private school, so until she got involved in the club none of the others knew her that well. But the more we know her, the more we like her. She's super-smart and fun to be around. Before Dawn left, Shannon was an associate member, which meant that she didn't come to meetings but was on call when we needed extra sitters. Now that she's a full (if temporary) member, the only associate member is Logan Bruno, who wasn't at our meeting that day.

Logan is Mary Anne's boyfriend. He's from Kentucky, and he has this sweet, Southern drawl. He's a sports nut, like me, so we get along well. Mary Anne can get pretty mushy about him. In fact, she tends to go on and on about how much he looks like — guess who? — Cam Geary!

Our club also has two junior members, Mallory Pike and Jessi Ramsey, who are both eleven instead of thirteen like the rest of us. They're best friends, but, like Mary Anne and me, they're opposites in certain ways. For one thing, they look nothing alike. Mal has red hair, freckles, glasses, and braces, while Jessi is African-American, with dark brown eyes and smooth dark skin. Mal comes from a huge family (eight kids!), while Jessi just has one sister, Becca, and one brother, John Philip (otherwise known as Squirt). Mal's mainly interested in reading and writing — she wants to write and illustrate children's books someday — and Jessi is a serious ballet student. Still, though they may not appear to have a lot in common, Mal and Jessi have major chemistry together. They're inseparable.

As a matter of fact, as that day's meeting wound up, Mal and Jessi were already plotting and planning their summer together. "I definitely want to spend some time at the movie set," said Jessi. "Even if we're sitting a lot, I bet sometimes we'll be able to bring our charges. It'll be awesome!"

Mal agreed. And so did the rest of us. The Day I Found Out It Was Going to Be an Interesting Summer was drawing to a close, but the real fun was just beginning.

CHAPTER 3

Trucks. Tons of big, huge, noisy trucks with heavy cables and wires running out of them. And vans and trailers and carts of all sizes loaded with complicated-looking equipment. And lots of people — I mean *lots* — all dressed in jeans and T-shirts and baseball caps, standing around looking like they weren't doing a thing.

That was my first impression of the movie set. It wasn't exactly what I had expected, but then I hadn't really known *what* to expect. All I knew was that I was supposed to be there at seven-thirty that Tuesday morning, to meet Derek for his first day of filming.

The film's main location was the elementary school, on the ballfield. The entire parking lot — and half the field — was packed with trucks and vans. I turned to Charlie, who was standing between Sam and me at the edge of the parking lot.

"I wonder where I'm supposed to go," I said.

He shrugged, peering at the scene. "I was wondering the same thing," he said. Charlie had landed a job on the set, as a gofer for the assistant-assistant stage manager.

Sam yawned. "I know where *I'm* going," he said. "That spot over near third base looks like the perfect place for a nap. I'm sure somebody will wake me up when things start happening." He loped off across the field.

Sam didn't have a job on the set — he had just come along to watch. Most of my friends were hoping to come, too. In fact, most of Stoneybrook would probably be on hand, since having a movie shot here was about the most thrilling thing that had ever happened in our town.

I was feeling just as sleepy as Sam. It was going to take awhile for me to adjust to getting up so early every day. But even though I was tired, I was also incredibly excited — and kind of nervous about what this job was going to be like. Just then, I saw a woman walk by with a clipboard under her arm. Somehow she looked official. "Excuse me," I said, "but do you know where I might find Derek Masters?"

"Isn't he one of the gaffers?" she asked.

Gaffer? What was *that*? "Um, no," I said. "He's an actor."

"Try makeup," she said, waving a hand toward the trailers. Just then, the walkie-talkie she wore at her waist gave a squawk.

"Which — " I began, but she was trotting off, talking quickly into her walkie-talkie.

"I'm going to head over there," Charlie said, pointing toward a cluster of people who were standing near home plate, gesturing and talking. "I think I see one of the guys I talked to about the job." He grinned at me. "Good luck," he said.

I stood there for a moment and tried to figure out what to do next. How would I ever find Derek in all this confusion? Another woman with a clipboard walked by, and I was about to stop her and ask her where makeup was when I heard someone call my name. I turned to see Derek waving at me as he emerged from a shiny black car with a uniformed chauffeur behind the wheel. Todd and Mr. Masters were climbing out behind him.

"Derek!" I said. "Hey, you must have grown about four inches." He had definitely sprouted since the last time I'd seen him.

Derek grinned and looked down at the ground. Mr. Masters smiled at me and shook my hand. "Good to see you, Kristy," he said. "Listen, we're running a little late. Derek should be in makeup by now, and I need to take Todd over to wardrobe to get his costume re-fitted."

"No problem," I said. "The only thing is, I don't know where — "

"I'll show you," said Derek. "It only *looks* confusing here. Once you get used to them, all movie sets are pretty much alike." He led me on a crooked course around the parking lot. We walked around the big trucks, stepping over the huge cables and dodging men with their arms full of electrical equipment. "Those are the gaffers," Derek said, after we'd nearly collided with one of them. "Electrical guys. Don't get in their way!"

"What are the big trucks for?" I asked. "And why do they make so much noise?"

"That's where the generators are," he said. "You know, to make all the power for the lights and stuff."

I nodded. I could see I had a lot to learn, but I had a feeling Derek could teach me. He seemed to be totally at home on the set.

"Here we are," he said, leading me up to one of the trailers. He pointed to a sign on it that said "makeup." The trailer had three doors, which weren't marked, but Derek just pushed open the middle one and walked in. I followed behind him.

"Missy!" said Derek, giving a high-five to a blonde woman in a pink smock. "I was hoping you'd be here." He turned to me. "Missy is the best makeup person in the business," he explained. Then he hopped into the seat in front of the mirror. "This is Kristy, Missy," he said. "She's kind of my assistant on this shoot."

"Pleased to meet you," said Missy. "Have a seat." She moved a stack of magazines from a stool and gestured toward it. I sat down and looked around. We were in a small cubicle — I guess the trailer had been divided into at least three of them — with a mirror along one wall. A shelf with piles and piles of makeup and hairspray and stuff ran under the mirror. The trailer was cool and comfortable, and I suddenly realized that it was air-conditioned. I relaxed and smiled. This was going to be a pretty neat job.

Missy got right to work. "Nothing fancy today," she said. "The vampires'll be getting fangs and blood and all that stuff, but you're just a regular kid. A little base, a little powder, a little work on the eyes, and you'll be all set. Then Nancy'll come in and do your hair."

I watched, amazed at how much stuff Missy slathered onto Derek's face to make him look like "a regular kid." Derek's eyes met mine in the mirror, and he smiled. "This is going to be a fun set," he said. "It's a neat script, too. Have you heard anything about it?"

I shook my head.

"It's about this kid who comes to America

as a foreign-exchange student from Transylvania. His name's Laddie Alducar, and he's a real charmer — everybody likes him. What they *don't* know is that he's a vampire, and he's been sent here by his parents to recruit more vampires."

"Who plays Laddie?" I asked. "Is it Cam Geary?"

"Nope," said Derek. "It's Carson Fraser — you know, that blond guy from *Miami Beach, USA*?"

I was pretty sure I could picture the actor, even though I hardly ever watched that show. He has longish, wavy blond hair and sleepy-looking blue eyes. I guess he's kind of a hunk, although he's not *my* type.

"Anyway," Derek went on, "in the movie, Laddie starts to wish he wasn't a vampire. He feels sad about how he missed out on a normal childhood — that's why he helps coach Little League games and stuff — and when he meets my character, we get to be friendly." He paused while Missy dabbed at his lips with a tiny sponge. "He can't decide whether to drink my blood or be like a big brother to me, but his vampire side wins out and he tries to recruit me. Some of his vampire pals help him out, too. Eventually, me and my friends figure out that he's a vampire — that Laddie is short for Vladimir and that his last name is Dracula with the letters rearranged — and there's this big final scene where we have to decide whether or not we should put a stake through his heart."

"Ew!" I said.

"Yeah," Derek agreed. "But there's a happy ending. Laddie ends up staying in America and becoming a normal kid."

By this time, Missy had finished and the hairdresser was fooling around with Derek's hair. Finally, both of them were done. "You'd better move your tail over to wardrobe," said Missy, giving Derek a hug. "They're waiting for you."

I followed Derek to another trailer, where a lady in a long gray smock with lots of pockets helped him get dressed in a Little League uniform that said "Tigers" across the chest. Then he led me back out into the chaotic set. "My scene was supposed to be filmed at ten," he said, checking his watch. "But I can tell they're running late. Let's grab a snack, and I'll show you around a little."

We headed for a truck with tables set up in front of it, near a circle of director's chairs. "They have fruit and cookies and juice and stuff here all day," Derek explained. "Then at noon they put out a big spread for lunch." He took an apple from a tray and thanked the woman behind the counter. "Want something?" he asked me. I shook my head. Derek headed for the group of chairs and took a seat. "This is where the actors can relax between takes," he said. "Whoa — don't sit in *that* one!"

I jumped up from the chair I had chosen and looked at it. In script across the back it said "Carson Fraser."

"We all have our own chairs," Derek explained. "And some people don't take it too well if you sit in theirs."

Just then, a tall blond guy walked up, with three girls trailing behind him. "Hey," he said to Derek, raising an eyebrow. "Bring me some soda," he said to one of the girls. The girl dashed to the snack table and came running back with a can of soda. She offered it to Carson — by now it was obvious to me that the blond guy was Carson Fraser — but he shook his head. "Not *that* junk," he said, when he saw the can. "Get me my usual." The girl looked as if she might cry.

I exchanged glances with Derek, and he gave me a secret grin.

Then a short bald man in a shiny black running suit came up to Carson, who was by then seated in his chair. He glanced at me and Derek dismissively, and then bent over and started to whisper in Carson's ear. "That's Frank Bottoms, his manager," Derek whispered to me. "He's really protective."

The manager straightened up and gave Derek an insincere smile. Just then, a woman wearing a red silk blouse, a short black skirt, and red high heels trotted up to Carson. "And that's the publicist for the movie," Derek whispered. "Sheila Mayberry. She's famous for getting tons of press on the movies she works on. And that guy who just walked up behind her is Cliff Chase, the movie's producer." He pointed out a man wearing expensive-looking black sunglasses.

I was fascinated. Just as I was getting ready to ask Derek three million questions about the set and the people on it, a guy with one of those clipboards came up to Derek and told him he was needed on the set. I followed Derek to the spot they'd prepared, surrounded by lights and cameras and a whole bunch of other equipment.

Across the way, I saw Mary Anne, Stacey, Logan, and Mal with the kids they were sitting for, including some of Mal's little sisters and brothers. I waved to them, and they all waved back, except for Claire, Mal's youngest sister. She was looking around nervously, and she must have missed seeing me. I saw Sam, too, and a girl from school named Cokie Mason, and a bunch of other people I knew from school. There were also some people I didn't know. I noticed one girl who was clutching a fan magazine with Carson's picture on the front. She had long, stringy blonde hair, and her cheeks were almost as red as the rose she wore in her buttonhole. She must have been really excited about having a chance to see Carson at work.

That day, as I stood around watching Derek at work, my admiration for him grew by the minute. He was completely and totally professional, and when they actually got around to shooting his scene with Carson — which seemed to take forever to set up — his acting was terrific. In fact, I thought he was a lot better than Carson. Carson was wearing dark sunglasses — since he was supposed to be a vampire he'd have to wear them all the time during daytime scenes — and he was acting extremely bored.

As for me, it was hard to imagine being bored on a movie set. I mean, it's true that I did a lot of standing around and waiting, but there was so much to look at and listen to. The first time I heard the director say "Action" (they really do say that!), I got little shivers down my back, and I knew right then I was going to *love* being on the set. This was definitely going to be the most exciting babysitting job I'd ever had.

CHAPTER 4

By eleven the next morning, my feet were really starting to kill me. I had learned by then that standing around doing nothing is one of the main activities on a movie set. Everybody does it. Why? Well, the thing is, every person on the set has a very specific job — for example, taking care of one certain light, or standing by with a powder puff to fix actors' makeup between shots — and when you're not doing your job, there's nothing to do but stand around and wait until you're needed.

I'd learned a few other things about movie sets, too. For one thing, I fit right in, fashion-wise. The only person I ever saw dressed up was Sheila Mayberry, the publicist. Just about everybody else — except the actors, when they were in costume — wore jeans, or shorts, and ratty T-shirts. That outfit, plus maybe a baseball cap, was practically the uniform for the set.

My other new moviemaking fact was this: they never film the scenes in sequence, the way you see them in the finished picture, so if Derek hadn't told me about the plot of the movie, I might never have figured it out. What filmmakers do is shoot all the scenes that take place in a certain location at once, to save money. That makes total sense, considering all the people and equipment that have to be moved around to each location. So, the scenes I was watching them shoot were not necessarily in any order (at least, not in any order that made sense to me). After they were finished with the scenes at the ballfield, the whole operation would move inside to the school gym, and then to that house near Mary Anne's. After all the Stoneybrook scenes were completed, the cast and crew would head for California, where they would shoot some final interior scenes in the studio.

Anyway, the scene they were shooting that day was one in which Laddie (Carson Fraser) was trying to trick Derek's character, whose name is Jason, into drinking his blood! Ew, right? Only it wasn't as bad as it sounds. It wasn't like he was opening a vein and telling Jason to drink up. Instead, he offers him what looks like cherry Kool-Aid, from a glass jar. The scene is supposed to be kind of light and funny, since Jason just keeps saying that he's not thirsty, or that he has some Gatorade of his own. Laddie keeps trying to talk him into drinking the blood, but he keeps being frustrated in his attempts. Lucky thing, of course, since if Jason drank the blood, that would be his first step on the way to becoming a vampire himself.

As I stood watching, I became more and more impressed with Derek's skill as an actor. Before each shot, the director (whose name is Harry) would walk up to Carson and Derek and chat with them for a while, telling them about what was supposed to happen in the shot and giving them specific instructions on how to say their lines. "Keep it light, here," he'd say to Derek, or "Don't give us too much — hold back for the next shot." Derek would nod, and when the cameras were rolling he would do exactly as Harry had told him.

Carson, on the other hand, seemed to spend a lot more time complaining about the way his costume fit than listening to Harry. Harry kept urging Carson to work on his accent, which was supposed to be vaguely Transylvanian, but Carson didn't seem to want to be bothered.

I was beginning to see that Derek pretty much upstaged Carson during any scene that featured the two of them. He wasn't doing it on *purpose*, I was sure of that. He understood that Carson was the star and that his was only a supporting role. It was just that he cared enough to give it his best shot, and his best shot beat Carson's lukewarm performance every time.

The real story that day, though, was not what happened during filming. It was what happened during the lunch break, as Derek and I were heading for the caterer's truck.

Remember how I noticed that Derek had grown since the last time I'd seen him? Well, apparently he hadn't quite gotten used to his new, gangly body; he didn't seem entirely comfortable in it. The first hint I had of this problem was when he climbed out of the limo that second morning, right after I had arrived on the set. Now, Derek's limo does have a driver, but he's not the kind of driver who steps out and opens the door for you. So when the car pulled up, Derek pushed open the door (he was alone, since Todd wasn't needed on the set yet) and climbed out. But instead of making a suave and movie-star-ish entrance, Derek stumbled over his own feet, nearly fell, grabbed the car door to catch himself, and ripped his sleeve on the latch.

"Derek, are you okay?" I asked, running over to him.

"I'm fine," he said, blushing, as he looked around to see if anybody else had noticed.

Not long afterward, when Derek was in makeup, he had another little accident. It involved the plastic cape that Missy had draped around him, and several cans, jars and bottles that were laid out on the shelf beneath the mirror — and it wasn't pretty. Missy was nice about it, though, even after she and Derek bumped heads as they both bent to pick up some of the stuff that had been swept off the shelf.

I watched Derek closely as we walked to the set, trying to make sure he didn't fall over any cables or knock any lights off their stands — but the trip was uneventful. Still, I was beginning to realize that Derek was in a very uncoordinated stage.

Because of that, I wasn't too surprised at what happened on our way to lunch. As we walked past the trucks and vans, Derek was explaining what each one was. "That's where the sound technicians work," he said, pointing out one truck. "And the carpenters keep all their stuff in this one." Then he ran up to a large red van parked near the caterer's truck. Big white letters on its sides said "Hill's Props." "This is the propmaster's van," he told me. "They always have really neat stuff here."

Sure enough, the back of the van was open, and I could see all kinds of fascinating items.

There was lots of baseball equipment, of course, but there was also stuff that I figured must be for shoots at other locations. I saw some rubber bats — not baseball bats, but the furry, flying kind — and a baby carriage, and a pile of fake fruit.

"Check this out," said Derek, picking up a beautiful stained-glass lamp. "I'm sure it's made of plastic, but it looks real, doesn't it? This must be for the scene in the professor's study, when my friends and I go to consult with him about vampires." He held it up over his head. "Like my hat?" he asked, grinning. The sun shone through the glass and made little colored spots — red, purple, and green — on his face.

"Derek — " I began. I was just about to tell him to be careful, when the lamp slipped out of his hands, fell to the ground, and shattered into what looked like a million pieces. "Oh, no," I moaned.

"I guess it wasn't plastic," Derek said. "Oops!"

"Oops?" roared a voice behind us. "You destroy a one-of-a-kind Tiffany lamp I spent six weeks trying to find, and that's all you can say? *Oops?*"

I turned around and saw a tall, skinny man with bright red hair and a face to match.

"Um, Kristy," said Derek, always polite,

"this is Zeke Hill, the propmaster. Zeke, this is — "

"I don't care *who* she is," Zeke shouted, "unless she's going to pay for that lamp or create another one on the spot. This is unbelievable. I *swore* I would never work on a set with kids again, but just this once I let Harry talk me into it. Cliff is going to have my head. I must have been nuts." He bent down and began to pick up shards of brilliantly colored glass.

"I'm really sorry, Zeke," said Derek, bending to help.

"Get out of here, kid," said Zeke. "And don't come fooling around my van again, got it?"

"Got it," said Derek, backing off. "Come on," he hissed to me. We made tracks for the lunch truck. Derek didn't say a thing about the lamp incident as we helped ourselves to sandwiches, soda, and cookies. I think he just wanted to forget all about it.

But five minutes after we sat down to eat, Sheila Mayberry came waltzing up in a pair of pink heels. That day she was wearing a gauzy pink blouse and silky black pants, and her hair was held back with rhinestone clips — pink, of course.

"Derek," she said, "I just talked to Zeke."

"Oh, great," said Derek, under his breath.

"Is he still mad?" he asked Sheila. "Is he going to tell Harry?"

"He was planning to, but I talked him out of it." She leaned forward and spoke in a confidential tone. "I don't want word to get out on this until *I* put it out."

"What are you talking about?" Derek asked.

"This is a great little story!" she said eagerly. "I'll plant some pieces in the trade magazines, and maybe in *People*, or *Newsweek*. The press will eat it up. It's a great human interest story — everybody can relate to clumsy, growing boys."

I was confused. "Won't that make Derek look silly?" I asked. "I mean, a story like that doesn't really reflect all that well on the movie, does it?"

"Let me tell you something, honey," said Sheila.

"Her name's Kristy," said Derek.

"We have a saying in P.R. — public relations, that is," Sheila went on. "It goes like this, Kristin — "

"Kristy," I said.

"Whatever," she said. "The saying is, 'There's no such thing as bad publicity.' And it's one hundred percent true, believe me."

"I don't get it," I said.

"She means that no matter what a story *says*, it brings attention to the movie," Derek explained. "And attention is always good."

"Yes, Derek!" said Sheila, sounding like a kindergarten teacher. "He's right," she added, turning to me. "My goal is to have *Little Vampires* on the tip of everybody's tongue by the time it airs on TV this fall. This business is all about ratings, and my job depends on good ones."

I nodded. "I understand," I said. But I wasn't sure I really did. The whole thing seemed a little ridiculous to me. But then, the movie set was like a whole different world, and I guess I shouldn't have been surprised that it had different rules. I was beginning to see that it was going to take me awhile to learn them all.

CHAPTER 5

Friday

Kristy, you are so lucky to have a job on the set. Talk about exciting! Plus, you're working with the best actor in the movie — everybody thinks Derek's doing a great job. The set is so cool. I'd be hanging out there every day, if I could. Unfortunately, I don't think that's going to be possible— not as long as I'm responsible for watching Claire in the mornings. She has a major case of vampire-phobia.

"**C**an we go? *Please? Pretty* please?" That was Margo, who was hanging on Mal's arm and pleading with all her might. (Seven-year-olds are good at that.)

"Let's go watch them make a movie — I know it will be totally groovy," said Vanessa, dreamily. Vanessa's nine. She wants to be a poet someday, and she practices by speaking in rhyme whenever possible.

"*I'd* like to go," said Mal. "But — " she nodded her head toward Claire, who was sitting on the living room rug, singing softly to herself. Claire, the youngest Pike, is five. "How about it, Claire?" she asked gently. "Want to go watch them make the movie?"

"No! No!" screamed Claire, suddenly upset. "I won't go, and you can't make me!"

Mallory was taking care of her three sisters that Friday morning, as she would be most mornings during the summer. Both of her parents were at work, and her brothers were playing soccer every day at the summer recreation program that meets in the park. (Mal has four brothers: Nicky, who's eight, and Adam, Jordan, and Byron, who are all ten — they're identical triplets!)

"What's her *problem*?" asked Vanessa, disgustedly.

"Her problem is that Adam and Jordan have

been filling her head with stories about vampires," said Mal, "and now she's so scared that she won't go near the set."

"Vampires suck your blood," said Claire. "They come and get you in the night, and bite your neck." She looked up at Mal, wide-eyed. "It's true, you know."

Mal sighed. "It isn't, really," she said. "It's just a story."

"No," said Claire stoutly. "It's true. Some people *think* it's just a story, but Adam said they're wrong."

Mal rolled her eyes. "Wait'll I get my hands on him," she muttered.

"Claire's ruining everything," said Margo, with a pout. "She's being a baby. Scaredy cat, scaredy cat!" she taunted, sticking her tongue out at Claire.

"Am not," said Claire.

"Can me and Margo go by ourselves?" asked Vanessa.

"No way," said Mal. "That set is full of trucks and people. I don't want you guys hanging out there without me." She walked over to the couch and sat down. "Claire, come sit on my lap for a minute," she said, patting her knees. "I want to talk to you."

Claire climbed up onto Mal's lap, and Mal took a deep breath. She told me later that it took everything she had to keep a patient,

44

understanding tone in her voice while she had a long talk with Claire about things that are real and things that are imaginary, and about why some people enjoy scary stories and others don't, and about how the vampires in the movies are only actors playing parts.

Finally, Mal convinced Claire that it would be safe to visit the set. By that time, of course, Mal was exhausted — but she was still determined to go. So were Vanessa and Margo.

Things were really hopping on the set by the time they arrived. Filming was being done inside the school that day, in the gym, since it was pouring outside. The scenes in the gym, Derek had explained to me, were supposed to be taking place at an end-of-the-season Little League party for players and their friends. In the movie, Carson's character, Laddie, brings a few "cousins" to the party — who are actually other vampires, sent from Transylvania to help him with his mission. They're very charming young men, and everybody at the party thinks they're wonderful.

Then, once the party is in full swing, the young men change into vampires — fangs, glowing red eyeballs, and all. They terrorize Jason (Derek) and his friends, and then swoop off into the night.

The guys who were playing the vampires were having a blast that day. This was their first time in full vampire makeup, and they couldn't seem to get enough of walking up to people and saying things like, "I vant to drink your blooood!" Harry, the director, was going nuts trying to make them settle down. Derek, who was, of course, in "normal kid" makeup, acted disgusted — although I had a feeling he might have been a little jealous.

He had just finished shooting his big scene of the day, in which Laddie interrupts while Jason is talking with a pretty red-headed girl. As usual, Derek had looked totally professional. At least, he looked professional right up until the end, when he ruined the shot by slipping and falling in the middle of the gym floor.

Harry was exasperated. "Masters," he said, "I never knew you were such a klutz. We're going to have to shoot that scene again. I'll squeeze it in next week, who knows where, but it can't be today. We're on a tight schedule here, and everybody else is already made up and ready for the next shot."

"But Harry," I heard Derek say, "it wasn't my fault. There was something spilled on the — "

But Harry had turned his back and was consulting with the lighting technician.

While we waited for the cameramen to set up for the next shot, Derek and I stood together in one corner of the gym. "I can't believe I fell," said Derek. "But there *was* something slippery on the floor. This time it really wasn't my fault."

"I know," I said, patting his shoulder. I could see he felt terrible about ruining the shot. I tried to think of some way to change the subject, but I wasn't having much luck — until I spotted Mal standing over on the sidelines with Margo, Claire, and Vanessa. "Hey Mal! Come here." I waved them over.

"Are you sure it's okay for the girls and me to be here?" Mal asked, as she approached us.

"Sure," Derek said. "If anybody asks, just tell them you're with me."

Mal looked around at all the lights and equipment. "This is so cool," she breathed. Then she turned back to Derek. "You were great in that scene, Derek," she said. "Are you, um, okay?"

"I'm fine." He looked embarrassed.

Claire seemed nervous, and I noticed she stayed close to Mal, but Vanessa and Margo were scanning the room eagerly. "Where's Carson?" Vanessa asked Derek. "I want his autograph."

I glanced at Derek, worried that he might feel slighted because Vanessa didn't want *his* autograph. But he seemed to understand that he was old news to the Stoneybrook kids.

"He's in makeup, having his fangs adjusted," said Derek.

"Fangs?" asked Claire, anxiously.

Before any of us could remind her that they were just fake fangs, something awful happened. One of the vampires came running through the gym door and swooped right up to Claire. "Hello, my pretty," he said, baring his fangs and letting his red eyes flash. "Care to dance?"

"Aaaah! Aaaah!" screamed Claire. She turned and raced out of the gym.

"What'd I do?" asked the vampire, bewildered. "I was just kidding around."

"Yeah, well, I guess you kidded around with the wrong kid," Derek said, shaking his head.

Mal grabbed Vanessa and Margo. "Come on, you guys!" she said. "We have to find her. 'Bye, Kristy! 'Bye, Derek!"

Vanessa and Margo followed Mal out of the gym, looking back at Derek and me with wistful glances.

By the time they were gone, the vampire had run off to find his next victim, and Derek and I just looked at each other and shrugged. "Another day on the set," said Derek. "I hope she'll be okay."

Claire *was* okay, Mal told me later. At least, sort of. She *did* manage to stop shrieking by the time they all got home. Vanessa and Margo weren't happy about leaving the set, and both of them stomped upstairs to sulk. But Claire headed straight for the kitchen and started to rummage through the cabinets. "Do we have any garlic?" she asked Mal.

"Sure," said Mal, helping her find it. "Why do you want it?"

"To keep vampires away, of course," said Claire. "Also, I need some water to throw on them if they come near me," she went on, filling a jar at the kitchen sink, "and a mirror, so I can hold it up and see if they have any reflection. If they don't, that *proves* they're vampires."

Claire spent the rest of the day on vampire patrol, according to Mal. She closed and locked her bedroom windows and got a wooden stake out of the garden, even though she wasn't exactly sure what she was supposed to do with it. Mal decided not to tell her about driving it through a vampire's heart, since she knew that would only freak Claire out. Claire also made sure she had a turtleneck shirt laid out to sleep in, since she figured the vampires couldn't bite her neck if they couldn't see it.

By the time Mal called me that night, all the Pikes were home and Claire was getting ready for bed. "I don't know when I'll be on the set again," Mal said, sighing. "And I don't know *how* Claire's going to shake her fear of vampires."

I sympathized. "I'm really sorry about what happened," I said. "So's Derek."

"Speaking of Derek," Mal said, "he is *such* a good actor. I heard a few people talking about him as I was leaving the set. This blonde girl said he was turning into even more of a star than Carson!"

"He *is* good," I said, feeling kind of proud, even though I had nothing to do with Derek's talent. Just then, I heard some muffled yelling over the phone line. "What's going on?" I asked.

"Oh, it's Claire and Margo," said Mal, sounding tired. "Claire's insisting on sleeping with the overhead light on in their room, and she and Margo are fighting about it. I better go."

I said good-bye to Mal and went to bed myself. I was exhausted after a whole week on the set. As I drifted off to sleep, I found myself remembering how, when I was little, I went through an awful phase of being afraid of mummies. I decided that I owed it to Claire to help her get over her fear of vampires — if only I could figure out a way.

CHAPTER 6

"It always makes me so nervous when he does his own stunts," said Mrs. Masters. She and I were sitting outside the makeup trailer; Derek was inside, being made up for Wednesday's shoot. The set was buzzing, as usual, with crew people running back and forth, gaffers setting up lights, and actors clustered near the caterer's truck across from us.

"But everybody says this one is totally safe," I said. "And Harry says it's the only way, since they need a closeup of Derek's face." I watched a guy in a Dodgers cap trundle a cart full of costumes through the crowd. Charlie trotted by with his hands full of wires and cables and waved to me with one pinky. I waved back.

"I know." Mrs. Masters sighed. "I'm sure it will be fine. But I still wish there was some way Cheryl could do it."

Cheryl is a stuntwoman. She's small, so she

works perfectly as a stand-in for Derek. She had already done some stunts for the other actors: flying on wires through the gym, for example, as one of the vampires. But that day, she wouldn't be needed.

Mrs. Masters had come to the set for the morning, even though I was there to watch Derek, and Claud was on hand to watch Todd who would be shooting his first scenes later that day. Mrs. Masters had told me that she always made it a point to be on the set when Derek was doing a stunt.

Derek's stunt that day was nothing too fancy. All he had to do was fall through a pane of glass. That may sound dangerous, but it really wasn't — or at least, that's what I had been told. See, the "glass" would actually be this stuff they call breakaway glass, which *looks* just like glass but shatters safely on impact.

The scene they were shooting was supposed to take place at the end of the party, when the vampires are going wild. When Derek's character tries to keep one of them away from a girl — the same red-haired girl "Jason" was talking to earlier — the vampire shoves him through a window. The shot would show Derek falling through the window in slow motion, with a closeup on his face.

"Isn't Derek ready yet?" That was Todd,

who had just popped out of his own makeup trailer, with Claudia in tow.

"He'll be done any minute," said Mrs. Masters.

"I'm thirsty," said Todd.

"Why don't you go get a soda?" asked Mrs. Masters. "We'll be right here." Todd ran over to the caterer's truck, and Mrs. Masters turned to Claudia.

"How do you like being on the set?" she asked.

"It's great!" said Claudia. "Missy just gave me a whole bunch of really cool makeup tips." She ran a hand through her hair. "Being a movie makeup person seems like a neat job."

"You'd be great at that, Claud," I said. "Or you could do costumes."

Claud nodded. "I'm going to ask Missy how you train for jobs like that."

Just then, three things happened at once. Derek came out of his trailer, looking spiffy. Mrs. Masters said, "Now where is Todd?" And I heard an unmistakable sound from behind me: the sound of glass shattering.

Claud and I stood up and turned to see what was going on. Three assistants with clipboards ran past us, toward the prop truck. "Oh, my lord!" said Claud, when she saw what had happened.

Todd was standing next to the prop van, looking stunned. Zeke Hill was alternately glaring at him and staring down at the ground, where a pile of glass shards lay around his feet. "I — I didn't mean to — " said Todd. Zeke's face was white this time, instead of red, but other than that he looked just the way he had the day Derek broke the lamp.

Mrs. Masters jumped up and ran over to Todd, with Claudia, Derek, and me right behind her. "What happened, baby?" she asked, bending down to hug Todd.

"I was just walking along kicking this rock," said Todd, "and then it went into the glass and broke it. I didn't mean to do it!" he said again. "It was an accident."

I looked at Zeke. Why wasn't he yelling? He was just standing there, shaking his head and looking bewildered — and shocked. "This shouldn't have happened," he said slowly.

"I'm so sorry," said Mrs. Masters. "We'll pay you for it."

"It's not that," said Zeke. "What I meant was, this was the pane of glass for Derek's stunt. It was supposed to be breakaway glass."

Suddenly, a light seemed to dawn in Mrs. Masters' eyes. "But if he had — " She stopped and put her hand over her mouth.

"That's right," said Zeke, nodding. "If Derek had fallen through *that*," he pointed at the pile of broken glass, "he could have been badly hurt." He shook his head again. "I just don't understand it," he said. "I *ordered* break-away glass, and that's what I received. I even double-checked it, just to be sure. Where did this other stuff come from?"

Derek and Todd were standing between me and Claudia, staring at the pile of glass. "Wow," breathed Todd.

"You can say that again," said Derek. He looked scared. I put my arm around his shoulders. I couldn't believe what a close call he'd had.

"I feel terrible," Claud whispered to me. "I was supposed to be with Todd."

"What's going on here?" roared a voice behind us. I turned to see Cliff Chase, the producer, elbowing his way through the crowd of people that had gathered.

"I don't understand it, Cliff," said Zeke. "This was breakaway glass, I know it was."

"Sure doesn't *look* like breakaway glass," said Cliff, nudging the pile with his foot. He looked over at Mrs. Masters, who was pale and shaken. He took her elbow. "It's all right," he said. "Derek wasn't hurt, and he's not going to be." Then he bent down and spoke to Derek. "I guess this is why the studio's lawyers don't like actors doing their own stunts," he said. "Don't worry, Derek. Cheryl's going to be taking care of all of your stunts from now on." Finally, he straightened up and turned toward Zeke. For a second, he just glared at him. The crowd grew quiet.

"You're fired," he said evenly. "I want you out of here. Now."

"But I — " Zeke began. His face was red again now. He looked completely humiliated.

"Now!" said Cliff. He turned away from Zeke, looking disgusted. He spoke quietly to the assistant at his elbow. "Call the agency," he said, "and get me another propmaster, pronto. I want somebody here by tomorrow." The assistant scurried off. Then Cliff turned to the crowd. "I'm shutting down the set for the rest of the day," he announced. "Shooting will start again tomorrow at eight." He gave one more disgusted glance at Zeke and stalked away.

The crowd stood silently for a second. Then one of the gaffers spoke up. "Tough luck, Zeke," he said.

"Yeah," said Zeke. He didn't look humiliated any more. Now he just looked angry. Some of the other workers tried to speak to him, but he brushed everybody aside and disappeared into his van.

"I don't believe it," said Claud. "How do you think that happened?"

"I can't imagine," said Mrs. Masters, who

was looking a little calmer by then, "but I have to admit I'm not sorry to see Zeke go. I never quite trusted him. He has a terribly short temper."

"Especially around kids," I said, remembering how he'd shouted at Derek.

"I don't know," said Derek. "I think Cliff could've given him a break. Why'd he have to *fire* him?"

Derek is *such* a nice kid.

"I don't think Cliff and Zeke get along all that well," Mrs. Masters said. "I've heard rumors about a feud between the two of them."

"Can we go home now?" asked Todd. "I want to try out that new Nintendo game we bought."

"Sure, honey," said Mrs. Masters. "But why don't you get that makeup off, first?" She sent the boys into their trailers and turned to Claud and me. "Claudia, please don't feel that this was your fault in any way. I was the one who told Todd to go get a drink. Maybe it was for the best, too. After all, if Todd hadn't broken that glass, Derek might have been badly hurt during his stunt. Anyway, I guess you two have the rest of the day off," she said. "Enjoy it!"

Claudia seemed relieved by what Mrs. Masters had said. Then she frowned. "I was kind of looking forward to being here," she said.

"It was going to be my first whole day on the set." Then she looked over my shoulder and her face brightened. "Hey, there's Stacey. She said she might come to watch today. Why don't we show her around a little?"

"You go on ahead," I said. "I'll catch up with you."

Claud yelled to Stacey and ran over to meet her. But I stayed put. There was something I needed to do.

I was pretty upset about what had *almost* happened to Derek. I had started to feel close to him, after being on the set with him all day every day — and now I felt super-protective. I needed to find out what had happened, and why. Had somebody *substituted* a pane of real glass for the breakaway glass? Or had the two just gotten switched by accident? If someone *had* done it, *why* had he done it? Was there somebody on the set who wanted to see Derek hurt? And if so, who could that somebody be? I needed to get to the bottom of this, just to set my own mind at ease.

I grabbed the first person-with-a-clipboard who walked by. "How can I find out more about where that pane of glass came from?" I asked her.

She shrugged. "I don't have anything to do with props," she said. "I work for Mr. Chase."

"Aren't there records and things?" I asked. "Receipts?"

"Sure," she began. "But — "

"Just show me where they are," I said. I guess something in my voice convinced her, because she led me to a trailer that was set up as an office and began to rummage through the papers on one of the desks.

"Hmmm," she said. "There's a bunch of delivery notices here, but mostly just for set materials and things." She showed them to me, and I noticed that the name on them was Rockaway and Sons, which is a local company. This movie was great for Stoneybrook businesses. I leafed through the stack, but nothing looked remotely suspicious. The assistant handed me another pile of receipts. "These are for props," she said, "but I don't see one for the breakaway glass."

I looked through papers for another few minutes, but soon I realized that I wasn't going to turn up any answers. The office was totally disorganized, and even if I knew what I was looking for I would probably never find it. I thanked the assistant and went to find Claudia and Stacey.

"Christine!" I heard a voice behind me call. I paid no attention, until somebody grabbed my arm. It was Sheila Mayberry, dressed all in lilac. Her eyes were sparkling with excitement, so I knew she must have heard about the incident with the glass.

"It's *Kristy*," I said, as politely as I could.

She took no notice. "Where's Derek?" she asked. "I need to talk to him." I steered her in the direction of makeup, and as I watched her trot toward the trailer in her lilac high heels, I shook my head. Even Sheila Mayberry couldn't make good P.R. out of what had happened on the set *that* day.

CHAPTER 7

"Unbelievable. I mean, this is really *unbelievable*." That was Frank Bottoms, Carson Fraser's manager talking. Charlie and I had arrived on the set early that day, the day after the incident with the breakaway glass. Derek was in makeup, and I was strolling around the set as I waited for him. I had just checked out the snacks at the catering truck — Derek wanted to know if they had chocolate chip cookies that day — and I was passing by the actor's lounge area when I heard Frank talking to Carson.

He was holding a newspaper and, as he spoke, he smacked the page with the back of his hand. "Mayberry had a field day with this one," he went on. "This really stinks." He glanced at the pile of other newspapers on a table next to him, and frowned.

"But, Frank," said Carson. "It's all just publicity for the project, isn't it?"

"Oh, yeah, sure," said Frank sarcastically. "More like publicity for a certain bratty little actor. When are *you* gonna get some press?"

"Maybe when I start breaking things," said Carson with a snicker.

Suddenly I realized what they were talking about. I guess I had been wrong in thinking that Sheila Mayberry would want to keep the glass episode quiet. She must have planted it in all the papers, and now Frank Bottoms was mad about Derek getting more publicity than his client — who was, after all, supposed to be the star of the movie. I tiptoed to a spot behind a van so I could hear some more without being seen.

"First he upstages you during your scenes together," said Frank. "And now he upstages you in the press. That brat is out to steal your show." He took a puff on his cigar. "We don't have to put up with it, either."

"What are we going to do about it?" asked Carson, leaning forward. "I mean, the way that kid kisses up to Harry, it's not a big surprise that he gets all the best closeups. And Mayberry obviously thinks he's something special, too."

"I'll take care of it, babe," said Frank gruffly. "You just concentrate on your acting. That's your job here."

"Well, okay," said Carson. "But let me

know if there's anything I can do. Like you keep telling me, this picture could *make* my career. I want to be sure it does. With my looks and talent, it shouldn't take much to make me a huge star."

How disgusting. He was obviously in love with himself, and he didn't seem to think there was room for another star on the set of *Little Vampires*. But I wasn't sure he was dangerous. He probably wasn't smart enough for that. Frank, on the other hand, might actually be able to think of some way to keep Derek from doing his job the way he *had* been doing it. Perfectly, that is.

I had a feeling Sheila Mayberry might have even more material to work with by the end of the day, and as a matter of fact, I turned out to be right. But I couldn't be *sure* that anything that happened was Frank's — or Carson's — doing.

Derek found me behind the van. I was still standing there, thinking, even though Carson and Frank had left the lounge area a few minutes before. "What are you up to, Kristy?" he asked. His cheeks looked pink, and I could see the powder on his face, but by now I knew none of the makeup would show on screen. It would just make him look normal, instead of washed-out by the lights.

"Just hanging out," I said. "Are they almost ready for you?"

Derek nodded. "They said five minutes. So, what about those cookies?"

"They have plenty of them," I said. "But your mom says you have to wait until after lunch to have any sweets."

"Bummer," said Derek, looking disappointed. "What good is being a movie star if you can't eat cookies whenever you want to?"

We headed over to the set, where they were almost ready to begin filming. That day's shooting was taking place in the gym again, and it involved some stunt work, which Cheryl would be doing. What they were filming that day was actually the scene *before* Derek goes through the window. (Remember how I said scenes are never filmed in sequence? Perfect example.) It was a scene in which one of the vampires picks Derek up, flies along with him for a moment, and then drops him from the highest point possible, right under the gym ceiling.

The special-effects people had rigged wires for Cheryl to "fly" on, and when Derek and I arrived on the set they were setting up her harness. Another stunt person — this one a man — was getting ready, too. He'd be doubling for the vampire.

Cheryl was wearing the exact same outfit as Derek — a red shirt and black jeans — and her short hair was combed just the way Derek's was. From the back, it was almost impossible to tell who was who.

"Good luck!" said Derek, giving the harness an envious look. I knew he would have given anything for the chance to fly.

"Thanks," said Cheryl. "Not that I'll need it, really. This type of stunt is totally routine. I could probably do it in my sleep."

The director's assistant called for Derek. The first shot that day would be a closeup of the vampire snatching him. Then the crew would work on setting up and shooting the stunt. I took a seat behind one of the casting assistants (I had heard they were on hand that day to audition extras for a crowd scene) and settled in to watch Derek do his stuff.

Unfortunately, as soon as I sat down, my view was blocked by somebody. It was that girl with the red rose in her buttonhole, the one I'd spotted on the set several times before. Her stringy hair was held back with barrettes, and she wore an old denim jacket over a flowered dress. She didn't look familiar to me, and I figured she must go to Stoneybrook High. She had walked up to the casting assistant, and she was talking earnestly to him. "Just a bit part," she said. "A walk-on, even. I don't care *what* it is, as long as I'm in this movie. Please? *Please?*"

"Well, we *are* looking for extras," said the assistant. "But I think we're looking mostly for younger kids — boys — at this point. Tell you what," he went on, "I'll take your name, and if we find out we need you, we'll give you a call."

The girl sounded pathetically grateful. "Oh, thank you, thank you," she said.

By that time, I was sick of craning my neck to try to see Derek. I got up and moved to another chair before I could hear the girl give her name. From my new seat, I could watch Derek closely and, as usual, I was incredibly impressed with his talent. The scene they were doing was really just one shot — of Derek's face as the vampire grabs him. But it was awesome to see Derek standing there listening to Harry's instructions, looking like a regular kid, and then watch how he could create an expression on his face within the next *minute*, an expression that summed up everything his character would be feeling upon being grabbed by a vampire. Watching Derek was really teaching me something about the art of acting.

When he finished, he came over to sit by me and watch the stunt. "Cheryl is so cool," he said admiringly. I agreed. She did look like a total professional. "I can't believe Harry wouldn't let me do this one," said Derek. "If that glass hadn't broken yesterday, *I'd* be the one getting clipped onto those wires. I was supposed to be doing this stunt myself."

"It's safer this way," I said, as we watched Cheryl and the other stuntperson being hoisted slowly up to the rafters. "I mean, what if something went wrong?"

Cheryl was about ten feet above us when suddenly there was a snapping noise. As we watched, horrified, one of the cables whipped around, the wires came loose, and Cheryl fell to the floor with a loud crash.

"Oh, no!" I shouted.

Derek jumped up and ran onto the set, along with me and Harry and a crowd of other people. "Are you all right?" he asked Cheryl.

She sat up and felt herself for broken bones. "I'm fine," she said slowly. "Just a little bruised."

"Get this equipment checked out!" Harry shouted to the crew. "I don't want to see any more accidents on this set, is that clear?"

People scurried about, checking wires and helping Cheryl out of her harness.

"Take five, everybody," said Harry in a weary voice. "We'll finish this shot after lunch."

Derek and I headed for the caterer's truck.

I could tell he was a little shaken, and I felt the same way. "Why was it *Cheryl's* harness that broke?" he asked. "It's like it was supposed to happen to me."

"I'm sure it was just a coincidence," I said. But to be honest, I wasn't sure at all. In fact, I was beginning to suspect that somebody was serious about hurting Derek. I just didn't want Derek to get upset, not when he had more scenes to film that day.

Later on, when filming had started again, I hunted down Charlie. "Have you heard anything about the accident?" I asked him.

He shrugged. "Somebody said they thought the cable might have been tampered with," he said. "But there's no way to be sure."

I nodded. That was exactly what I had suspected. Cheryl's "accident" was no accident. But as terrible and scary as it was, it wasn't the worst thing that happened that day.

Later that afternoon, after the flying scene had been shot without any further incidents, Derek was in the midst of a scene with the red-haired actress. At one point, when there was a break in the action, he ran over to me. "Kristy!" he said. "Can you go to my dressing room and get my breath mints? They're in a little cabinet next to the door. I ate some onions on my hamburger at lunchtime, and I have a feeling my breath really stinks."

"Sure, Derek," I said. I headed for his dressing room, which was in a trailer behind the caterer's truck. The trailer was divided into three rooms, just like the makeup trailer, and Derek's was in the middle. I pushed the door open and looked for the cabinet he had mentioned. But something else caught my eye first.

It was an envelope, addressed to Derek, propped up on the counter beneath the mirror. Now, ordinarily I would *never* open somebody else's mail, but in this case, something told me that I should. I picked it up and felt its weight, trying to decide if I really should open it. Then I took a deep breath and ripped it open.

I gasped. There was a heavy white card inside, with writing all over it. And the writing looked like it had been done in blood! Deep red scrawls covered the card, and red drips ran down from each word. "Scared yet?" the message said. "You *should* be. Get off this set — and *stay* off!" It was signed with a big red question mark.

I stuck the card and the envelope in my pocket, grabbed Derek's mints from his cabinet and hurried back to the set, thinking hard the whole time. Later that day, when Derek was finished with his scenes, I headed home and phoned Mrs. Masters. I told her about the note, and she thanked me for my concern. "I'll let Derek's agent know about it," she said. "This type of thing happens sometimes on movie sets, and he'll know what to do." She seemed a little worried, but not too upset.

After I finished that call, I made a few more calls — to every member of the BSC. "I'm calling an emergency meeting," I said to each of them. "Be at Claud's at seven!" It was time for the BSC to deal with the mystery on the set.

CHAPTER 8

"The thing is," I said, "there's no question in *my* mind anymore that somebody is out to get Derek."

My BSC friends and I were all settled into our regular places in Claudia's room, but this was no regular meeting. And, looking around the room, I could see that everyone else was just as concerned as I was about the trouble on the set of *Little Vampires*. Mary Anne was sitting on Claud's bed, between Claudia and Stacey. All three of them were listening intently. Shannon sat at the foot of the bed, taking notes in a small notebook. Jessi and Mal were on the floor, looking up at me with worried expressions. And Logan was leaning against Claud's desk, his arms folded and a concerned look on his face. (He never seems too comfortable at meetings — I guess because he's the only boy — and he always looks as though he might bolt out of the room at any minute.)

It was quarter after seven, and I had spent the past fifteen minutes filling everyone in on the latest developments. Of course, they had heard plenty from me before that night about what it was like to be on the set every day, but I had never given them all the details about the string of "accidents." Claud had seen one of them for herself, but she was shocked to hear about what had happened since then.

She passed a pack of Starbursts to Jessi and Mal. "Have some of these," she said. "I just lost my appetite."

"I think you're right, Kristy," said Shannon, looking serious. She checked over her notes. "The incident with the breakaway glass *could* have been a freak accident, and Cheryl's fall, too. But that note? That's definitely no accident."

Mal gave a shiver. "Did it really look like it was written in *blood*?" she asked. "That is so gross."

"Gross, and scary, too," said Stacey. "Who would *do* a thing like that?"

"That's the sixty-four-thousand-dollar question," I said.

"What?" everybody asked at once.

I blushed. "Oh, that's just something Watson says. I think it's from some old quiz show.

Anyway, all I meant was that *who* did it is exactly what we have to figure out. Otherwise, how can we stop them?"

"And they have to be stopped *soon*," said Logan. "Or else Derek could really get hurt."

"Exactly," I said. "And protecting Derek has to be our first priority. We can't count on his agent to help, since he's not even on the set."

"So now that we have a real mystery on our hands, how do we solve it?" asked Mary Anne.

Claud leaned forward, her eyes sparkling. "Well, if I were Nancy Drew," she said, "I'd suggest drawing up a list of possible suspects."

"Just what I was thinking," said Shannon. She held up her notebook. "And I've already started. Number one, *I* think, has to be that self-centered blond guy. The star who's so worried about Derek getting more attention. What's his name? Carter?"

"Carson," I said. "But I think Frank Bottoms, his manager, is a more likely suspect. He'd probably love to see Derek quit the movie."

"I'll write them both down," said Shannon.

"Good," said Claudia. "It never pays to eliminate suspects too early in the game."

"What about the guy who does — did — the props?" asked Stacey. "I mean, he's been fired, and he might be blaming Derek. Plus, he's probably mad at the producer, and he might be out for revenge. If he pulls enough tricks, the movie might have to be canceled." She nibbled at the apple she'd brought.

"Good!" said Shannon, scribbling madly in her notebook. "What's the propmaster's name again, Kristy?"

"Zeke Hill," I said.

"But hasn't he left town by now?" asked Jessi.

"According to what Charlie's heard, no," I said. "Apparently he's holed up in a local motel, hoping Harry will convince Cliff Chase to re-hire him."

"Okay," said Shannon, noting down Zeke's name. "I guess we'll have to try to track him down. Next?"

"I can't think of anybody else," said Mary Anne. "Or, rather, it seems like almost *anybody* could be a suspect. I mean, maybe it's not only Carson who's jealous of the attention Derek's attracting. One of the other actors might be out to get him."

"Yeah," said Logan. "Or maybe it's one of Zeke Hill's assistants, acting out of loyalty to his boss."

"For that matter, it could even be Cliff Chase," said Stacey, "although I don't know why he'd want to sabotage his own movie."

"He could have his reasons," said Mal darkly. "You never know."

"That's the problem," I said. "You never know. But if we try to keep track of every single person on that set, we'll go nuts. Plus, it'll take forever. I bet there are at least sixty people involved in making that movie."

"You're right," said Claudia. She seemed to have regained her appetite, since she was munching on a Kit-Kat. "I think what we need to do is narrow the field down to a few likely suspects, and keep a close eye on them. We won't *eliminate* any suspects, though. Then, if nothing pans out with the first people, we can start thinking about the others." She took a huge bite of Kit-Kat and smiled a chocolate-y smile. "That's what Nancy would do," she added.

"I can think of one possible suspect you guys haven't even mentioned," said Shannon.

"Really?" I asked. "Who?" I was sure we had thought of everybody.

"That P.R. lady," said Shannon. "The one you said is always so dressed up."

"Sheila Mayberry?" I asked. "Why on earth do you think *she* might be a suspect?"

"Think about it," said Shannon. "Didn't she tell you that her job depends on this movie earning big ratings? And didn't she say there's no such thing as bad publicity?"

"Wow!" said Mal. "You mean you think she might actually be *creating* these incidents, just so she can write stories about them and send them to the papers?"

Shannon nodded. "I know it sounds crazy, but face it, whoever is doing these things probably *is* a little crazy, right?"

"You might be onto something there," I said slowly. Sheila Mayberry still seemed like a totally unlikely suspect, with her matching outfits and fancy high heels, but what Shannon was saying did make a certain kind of sense. Absently, I picked up the pack of Starbursts and found a yellow one. I popped it into my mouth. "Sheila Mayberry, huh? Well, you better add her name to your list." I had to admire Shannon's deductive reasoning. She's so smart, and not just in school. She's just a plain old good thinker.

"I already did," admitted Shannon. We all laughed.

Then Logan turned serious again. "One thing we haven't really discussed," he said, "is whether this person really is out to get Derek, or if they are just creating random accidents and Derek's been unlucky enough to be involved in a few of them."

"You mean, this person just wants to mess

up the movie, and doesn't really care who he's hurting?" Jessi asked.

Logan nodded. "After all, the stuntwoman — Cheryl? — was the one who took that fall. Maybe it's just a coincidence that she was doing Derek's stunt."

"But what about that letter?" I asked. I was going to have a hard time forgetting those bloody-looking words. That note had really given me a scare.

"You know what I think?" said Stacey. "I think even if Logan is right, it doesn't really matter. The fact is, if somebody's out to hurt people — *any* people on that set — Derek is in danger. And we have to make sure he's safe."

"Definitely," I said, feeling that protective urge again. "I, for one, will be keeping a *very* close eye on him."

"I think the rest of us should try to spend more time on the set, too," said Mary Anne. "If more of us are there, and if we're all keeping our eyes open, we may come across some clues."

"I'll be there for the next few days," said Claudia. "Todd has a bunch of scenes coming up."

"Maybe the rest of us can go down there with kids we're sitting for," said Stacey.

"As long as you're not sitting for Claire," Mal said. "She still refuses to go anywhere *near* that set!"

I had forgotten all about the Claire problem. I'd been too swept up in the mystery on the set. I resolved again to work on helping her overcome her fears, but I knew curing Claire's vampire-phobia would have to wait until I was sure Derek was going to be okay. For now, Derek's safety would be my first priority. And it was good to know that my friends would be looking out for him, too.

CHAPTER 9

Tuesday

You know, guys, I hate to say it, but sometimes I almost miss school. I mean, school can be so much easier than real life. If I'm in science class and the teacher wants to know what kind of rock comes from volcanoes, the answer is easy to find in a book. But in real life, the answers don't come so easily. This Little Vampires mystery has me beat. In fact, it even has our best junior detective, Charlotte, totally stymied!

"It's almost like that movie set has a curse on it," said Charlotte, as she waved her bubble wand. She watched the bubbles float off toward an apple tree. "I keep seeing articles in the paper about all the accidents happening there. I'm worried about Derek."

"I've seen those articles, too," said Becca. "And everybody in town is talking about what's going on. Do you really think there's a curse?" She blew a stream of bubbles that followed Charlotte's.

"Oh, come on, you guys," said Shannon, who was sitting nearby on the grass. "There are no such things as curses. There are more rational ways to explain the accidents that have been happening."

Shannon was over at Charlotte Johanssen's house for a sitting job, and Charlotte had invited her best friend Becca — Jessi's little sister — over for the afternoon. They're both eight, and they have lots in common. Both of them are on the shy, quiet side and both of them love to read.

It was a hot, still day, perfect for blowing bubbles. Somehow, though, Shannon had a feeling the bubbles wouldn't keep the girls occupied for long.

Sure enough, about five minutes later Charlotte put down her bubble wand. "I'm bored," she said.

"Me, too," said Becca, blowing one last bubble.

"Besides," said Charlotte, with a grin, "I don't know what we're doing blowing bubbles when there's a mystery to be solved."

Shannon smiled. She knows Charlotte loves to play detective. In fact, Charlotte has helped the BSC solve a couple of mysteries in the past. Shannon had figured it was only a matter of time before Charlotte went to work on this case, too.

"Yeah," said Becca. "Isn't there something we can *do*? If Derek's in trouble, I want to help."

"Hmmm," said Shannon. She was thinking about the threatening note I'd found. *That* hadn't been reported to the paper. Shannon wondered for a minute whether it would be safe to involve the girls. "I don't know," she said slowly.

"Oh, please, Shannon?"

"Please?"

Shannon looked at the two pleading faces and made up her mind. After all, the accidents had all happened to cast or crew members. It was unlikely that the girls would be targeted. "Okay!" she said.

Both girls jumped up. "All *right!*" said Becca.

"Yesss!" shouted Charlotte. "So what do we do?"

"I have exactly the right job for us," said Shannon. "We'll tail the suspects."

"I'm good at that," said Charlotte. "I've done it lots of times. It's easy."

"Well, it may not be so easy this time," said Shannon. "There are a lot of suspects."

"Let's make a list," said Becca. "Isn't that what you have to do first?"

"Actually, I already have one," said Shannon, pulling her notebook out of her backpack. She showed the girls the list she had made during our emergency meeting.

"Carson Fraser?" asked Charlotte. "*He's* on the list? I thought he was a big star!"

"He is," said Shannon, "But he may be jealous because Derek's getting so much attention."

"And who's Frank Bottoms?" asked Becca.

"He's Carson's manager," Shannon explained, "and he's very protective of his client." She ran her finger down the list and explained who Zeke Hill was, and how he wasn't actually on the set anymore. Then she told the girls about Sheila Mayberry. "She's *my* number one suspect," Shannon said. "I definitely intend to keep an eye on her. I'm not exactly sure what she looks like, but judging from what Kristy says, we won't have any trouble spotting her. Her clothes really set her apart."

"Great," said Charlotte absently. She was staring at the list and biting her lower lip, thinking hard. A second later, she stood up, a determined look in her eyes. "I think the first thing we should do is go check out the motels on the edge of town. There are only three of them — it won't be hard to find Zeke Hill. And we can ride our bikes there." She pointed to the three bikes in the driveway: Shannon and Becca had both ridden over.

"But after that, we'll go to the set, right?" asked Becca.

"Definitely," said Charlotte.

Shannon laughed. It looked as if the girls were off and running, and her role was just to follow them. "Okay, then, let's go!" she said.

"Hold on," said Charlotte. "I'll be right back." She ran into the house and came back out with three pairs of sunglasses. "These'll help disguise us," she said. "Plus, they'll help us blend in with all those movie people."

"Good thinking," said Shannon gravely. Keeping a straight face, she chose a pair with pink hearts on the corners. Becca took the blue-and-white striped pair, and Charlotte slipped on a pair with sparkling rhinestones all over them.

Charlotte grabbed her bike. "Ready?" she asked.

As Charlotte had said, there are three motels on the outskirts of Stoneybrook. There's the George Washington (I always wonder if he was supposed to have slept there!), the Sleepy Bear, and the Kozy Kabins. Shannon and the girls checked out the Kozy Kabins first, but there was absolutely no action there. The Sleepy Bear was busier. A salesman was lifting suitcases into his car outside room 10, and a family with four kids — two of them screaming toddlers — was unloading their overstuffed van. But Zeke Hill was nowhere in sight.

Shannon and the girls hit pay dirt at the George Washington. First, Shannon spotted Zeke's van in the parking lot. Then, when they crept up to peer through a row of bushes that shielded the pool, they saw a red-haired man lying on one of the lounges. "That must be him," hissed Shannon. "Look, he has a phone right next to him. I bet he's waiting to hear from the director."

"He looks more like he's sleeping," whispered Becca, with a giggle. "I think I can even hear him snoring."

"Well, whatever he's doing, he's not creeping around making trouble on the set," said Charlotte. "But somebody else may be. Let's go!"

They rode over to the elementary school, where filming had moved back outside. The scenes being shot that day were of a community picnic at the ballfield, and there were lots of extras on hand. The casting people had rounded up a whole bunch of Stoneybrookites, promising them a good lunch and a possible shot at a few seconds on the screen. Stacey was there with the Perkins girls, and Mary Anne had brought Matt and Haley Braddock.

I had my hands full watching Derek that afternoon, since between each take he was mobbed by kids and their parents who wanted autographs. Even with Claudia's help (she was there to take care of Todd) there were times I lost sight of him. Plus, I kept being distracted by Cokie Mason. Even though we've never gotten along, that day she was acting like we were best friends. Ugh! She followed me around, begging me to introduce her to Carson Fraser. And when she wasn't bothering me, she was making a fool of herself trying to attract his attention. Every time she was anywhere near him, she would smile and pose and let out these loud, fakey giggles. It was embarrassing.

I was relieved when Shannon, Charlotte, and Becca arrived, since I figured they could help me keep an eye on Derek. "Hi!" I yelled, waving them over. But they pretended not to see me. "What's with them?" I asked Claudia.

"I bet they're playing detective," said Claudia. "Notice the sunglasses?"

I nodded. "You must be right," I said. "Okay, I'll pretend I don't know them. Maybe they'll pick up some clues."

Later, I found out that Shannon felt terrible about ignoring me. "Charlotte insisted on it," she explained. "She said if we talked to you we would 'blow our cover.' Sorry!"

Shannon and the girls spent the whole afternoon on the set, tailing first one suspect and then another. Becca was a little starstruck, and kept getting distracted when the actors walked by, but Charlotte was very intent on her detective work.

"There's Carson Fraser," she said. "And that must be his manager — the one talking to him." Carson was emerging from his dressing room, with Frank Bottoms (Shannon knew it must be Frank, from my description) trailing behind him. "Quick! We can follow them both," said Charlotte. She fell into step behind Carson and Frank, and Becca and Shannon followed her. Carson and Frank were deep in conversation, but it was impossible for Shannon and the girls to hear what they were saying.

As they neared the set, Frank and Carson separated. "You follow him," Charlotte hissed, pointing Shannon and Becca toward Frank. They stopped where Frank did, near the catering truck, but Charlotte kept up with Carson. Shannon kept half an eye on Frank, but she also watched Charlotte — after all, she thought, she *was* Charlotte's baby-sitter. Charlotte marched right after Carson as he walked past the makeup trailers, past wardrobe, past the circle of cameras and lights — and onto the set!

Shannon watched in horror as Harry, the director, stood up and cupped his hands around his mouth. "Little girl!" he yelled. "Hey! Little girl! No extras on the set right now, please. We're about to shoot a very important closeup."

Charlotte turned toward Harry and pointed at herself. "Me?" she asked. Her face was beet red.

"Yes, you!" he yelled. "Off the set, please."

Charlotte slunk back to where Shannon and Becca were waiting. "Why didn't you *warn* me?" she asked miserably.

"Sorry! I didn't know," said Shannon. Then, trying to help Charlotte over her embarrassment, she said, "But hey, in those sunglasses, you looked like you *belonged* in front of the cameras."

Once Charlotte had recovered, the three of them went in search of Sheila Mayberry. Before long, they spotted a woman Shannon was *sure* must be Sheila, because of her fancy jade-green outfit, near the makeup trailer. She was deep in conversation with Missy, the woman who does Derek's makeup. Charlotte whispered to Shannon that she thought the two of them might be plotting Derek's next accident. But as the girls drew nearer, all they heard was Missy telling Sheila about a new blusher she'd discovered. That was the last straw for Charlotte. "I've had it," she said to Shannon. "We picked the wrong day to come. There hasn't been one accident, and nothing suspicious happened. I'd rather go back home and blow bubbles." So, as Shannon reported later in the club notebook, after a whole day of sleuthing, the mystery on the set was still just that — a mystery.

CHAPTER 10

"Boy, did I need that day off," I said to Charlie, as we drove to the set two days later.

"Don't rub it in," said Charlie, yawning. "A day off sounds great, but there's no such thing for the crew *I* had to work yesterday."

There had been no filming the day before while the crew relocated. Harry was done with the scenes at the elementary school, and now he was ready to put in a few days filming at the house in Mary Anne's neighborhood. I had spent the day before lazing around, enjoying both the free time and the chance to take a rest from keeping an eagle eye on Derek. Mrs. Masters had phoned me to say that Derek's agent had said not to worry, but that wasn't so easy for me. We were still no closer to solving the mystery of who was out to get Derek, so while I was on the set, all I could do was watch him, and try to prevent any *more* accidents.

As soon I arrived on the set, I spotted Claudia. "Hi!" I said. "Are Derek and Todd here yet?"

"Nope," she said. "But I think we're early. I can't believe I'm actually getting up at six every morning during summer vacation!" She yawned and smiled.

I looked around the set. The house they were using is an old white one, with green shutters. It's a little rundown looking, which might be why the location scouts picked it for the movie. I remembered that an old man used to live there all alone, but now it looked as though the house was empty and waiting to be sold. The front yard and porch were where the shooting would take place, and the big side yard was totally full of people and equipment. Not every truck and van had been brought over (some were still parked at the elementary school) so it was kind of a mini-version of the set I'd gotten used to.

"Hey, here comes Derek's car." I pointed to the black sedan that was pulling up to the curb. Derek opened the door, and he and Todd jumped out. "Thanks, Mr. Mead," said Derek to the driver. "See you later!"

Derek and Todd walked over to join me and Claud. "He's great," said Derek, waving as Mr. Mead pulled away. "He used to be a prizefighter! This morning he showed me how to throw a right hook."

"Cool," I said. "But I think right now you'd better throw a right *turn* and head into makeup. Missy's waiting for you." I steered him gently toward the makeup trailer.

"We'll be over by the catering truck," said Claud. "Todd doesn't have a scene until later this afternoon."

Just then, over Claud's shoulder, I saw Cokie Mason approaching. "Don't look now," I whispered, "but here comes trouble."

Cokie minced up to us on white high-heeled sandals. She was wearing a white, ruffly peasant blouse that was pulled off her shoulders, and a pink flowered skirt. She looked ridiculous.

"Isn't it great to be here early?" she asked. "I just spotted Carson on his way into makeup. He was wearing a black t-shirt, and he looked just — " she sighed, as if she couldn't find the words to describe Carson's gorgeousness.

"Are you working here today?" I asked, knowing she wasn't — not dressed like *that*.

"Oh, no," she said. "I just came to watch."

I couldn't believe she didn't have anything better to do with her time than hang out on the set day after day, trying to catch Carson's attention. Claud and I exchanged glances.

"Well, I better go check up on Derek," I said, edging away. I felt bad leaving Claudia alone with Cokie, but I knew Claud could take care of herself. "See you later!"

I went into the makeup trailer and watched as Missy put the finishing touches on Derek's face. As she powdered him, he told me about the scenes scheduled for that day. "The house is supposed to be abandoned, and Laddie has started to use it as a clubhouse. He invites all the boys from the neighborhood to hang out there, in hopes of recruiting them as vampires. In the scene this morning, he tries to convince me to be his blood brother — but I refuse, since I already suspect he's a vampire. Then, this afternoon, we'll shoot this, like, club initiation scene with all the boys. That's the one Todd is in."

"You're all set, hon," said Missy, planting one last puff of powder on Derek's cheeks. "Break a leg out there today!" She covered her mouth. "Oops," she said. "Maybe I shouldn't say that to you. Sorry!"

Derek laughed. "That's okay," he said. "I think my luck is changing. I haven't had an accident in almost a week!" I was glad he could joke about it. Derek seemed oblivious to the fact that he might actually be in danger on the set, and I was happy to keep him in the dark.

We headed over to the space set up for the actors' lounge, where Claudia and Todd were waiting. Carson and Frank were there, too, but when Derek said hello, Carson barely acknowledged him. A bunch of other actors were sitting around, plus the usual hangers-on, like the blonde girl with the rose in her buttonhole.

"Aren't we supposed to be starting soon?" Derek asked Carson.

"Shooting's delayed," said Carson. "One of those jerky gaffers blew up a light or something."

Just then, I heard a loud and very fake-sounding giggle. *"There* you all are," said Cokie, sweeping into view. She glanced at Carson and blushed. He ignored her.

"I just wanted to make a brief announcement," said Cokie, wringing her hands nervously. "You're all invited to a party at my house, on Saturday night. Cast, crew, *everybody* who's working on the movie is welcome to attend." She giggled again, and I figured she was relieved to have made it through the little speech she must have memorized. "We have a pool," she added, "so bring your bathing suits! And bring a big appetite, too, because I'm going to have *tons* of food!"

"Sounds great," said Derek.

"Wonderful," trilled Cokie, but her smile

was even phonier than usual. She glanced once more at Carson, but he didn't meet her eye.

"I'll check his schedule," Frank Bottoms promised, smiling at Cokie. Carson shot him a dirty look. He obviously couldn't have been less interested in attending a party thrown by some local middle school girl.

Cokie pouted. Claud looked over at me and rolled her eyes. I rolled mine back. Cokie was too much. It was so obvious she was throwing the party just so she could say that a bunch of stars — especially Carson, of course — had been at her house.

As soon as she flounced away, Claudia leaned over to me. "Should we go?" she asked. "I mean, I guess we're included in that invitation."

"No way!" I said. "A party at Cokie's? You couldn't *drag* me there!"

So, guess where I was, two days later? That's right! I was sitting on a lounge chair, next to Cokie Mason's pool. Claud and the other BSC members had reminded me that if Derek was going, I should go. That way, I could keep an eye on him. It had been an accident-free week at the set, but I still didn't feel like I could let down my guard. Claudia had agreed to go with me, and by Saturday afternoon we had both actually started to look forward to the party. After all, we figured, it would be a gas to see who showed up, and to watch Cokie do her hostess act.

"Cokie's outdone herself," Claud whispered to me, gesturing to the decorations. There were pink lanterns strung all around the pool, and bouquets of pink flowers on the tabletops. Pink crepe paper dangled from every bush, and there were pink cups, pink plates, and pink napkins.

"Did I ever mention that I can't stand pink?" I whispered back.

It was a nice, warm summer night, and Cokie had provided the promised "tons" of great food. Claud and I hung out by the pool, eating hamburgers. I was wearing my usual: shorts and a T-shirt. Claudia was looking great in a loose, flowery jumpsuit. And Cokie? Well, Cokie was wearing a tight mini-dress (pink, of course), pink heels, and nail polish and lipstick to match.

"What *planet* is she from, anyway?" Claud whispered to me, as we watched her walk by carrying a tray loaded with potato salad and other goodies.

I gave a little snort. "Planet Weird," I said, helping myself to a deviled egg from a nearby platter. "Notice who hasn't shown up yet?" Carson was nowhere in sight. Instead, the pool area behind Cokie's house was packed with gaffers, makeup artists, and a lot of the younger actors. I giggled. "Guess the whole thing was a waste, as far as Cokie's concerned," I said. "At least Derek and Todd are having a good time."

Derek was, at that moment, about to do his fourteenth cannonball from the diving board. Todd was waiting his turn. Just as Cokie walked by, Derek bounced on the board, grabbed his knees, and gave a Tarzan yell as he plummeted into the water.

There was a huge splash, and Cokie jumped back — a second too late. She was *soaked*. Big dark blotches covered her mini-dress, and her hair, once so carefully curled, hung wetly around her face. Claud and I stifled giggles.

"Sorry!" Derek said, hoisting himself out of the pool.

Cokie looked like she wanted to kill him, but she quickly pasted on one of those phony smiles. "That's okay," she said. "As long as you're having fun." Then she turned and dashed into the house.

"Guess she has to make some repairs," Claudia said. "In case you-know-who really appears."

Well, Carson never did show up. The rest of us enjoyed ourselves, though, pigging out on the food Cokie had provided and dancing to the tapes she had made. "Great party, Cokie," I said, as Claud and I left. She looked tired and disappointed, and I suddenly felt a little sorry for her. "Anybody who didn't come really missed out," I added, trying to make her feel better.

But as it turned out, I was wrong. Anybody who didn't go to Cokie's party really *lucked* out. Why? Because almost everybody who *did* go got sick! I spent most of Sunday lying on the couch with an upset stomach and a pounding headache. Claudia was totally miserable, too. So were Derek and Todd, as I found out when I called the Masterses' house to check up on them.

"Do you think Cokie *poisoned* you all?" asked Mary Anne, when I talked to her later that day. "Maybe *she's* the one who's after Derek. After all, if she thinks so much of Carson, maybe she'd like to see Derek out of the picture, so Carson would get more attention."

It seemed ridiculous, but in fact the same thing had occurred to me. *Was* it Cokie who was after Derek? If not, who was it? I promised myself, as I lay there on the couch holding my stomach and moaning, that as soon as I felt better I would do everything I could to find out who was after Derek, and why. And then I'd make sure he was stopped, before something worse than a stomachache happened to him.

CHAPTER 11

By Monday, I had totally recovered. My headache was gone, and I felt like eating again. In fact, at the beginning of our BSC meeting that afternoon I was munching happily on a Twix bar Claud had given me, when the phone rang. "Mmmph!" I said. I gulped and swallowed. "I mean, I'll get it!" I grabbed the phone.

It turned out to be Mrs. Masters, calling to let me know that both she and Mr. Masters would be on the set the next day. She told me that Claudia and I were still welcome to be there, but that we didn't *have* to come.

"Terrific," I said, as I hung up. "This will give us some time to do a little sleuthing. Who wants to come?"

"Will you be on the set?" Mal asked.

"Part of the time, probably," I said. "Why?"

She sighed. "Because I'll be watching Claire," she said, "and if you're going to be spending time on the set, that means I can't come. Oh, well."

Mary Anne had a sitting job, and so did Logan and Jessi, but Stacey, Claud, and Shannon were all free and excited about doing some investigating.

We met the next morning, as we had planned, at the offices of John Rockaway and Sons, the contractor whose receipts I'd seen the day of the incident with the glass. Claud, using her deductive reasoning techniques (courtesy of Nancy Drew), had figured we might find some clues there. "After all," she'd said, "that pane of glass had to come from *somewhere*, and that company is as good a place to start looking as any. If they *did* supply it, maybe they can check their files and tell us who ordered it, and we'll have our culprit."

We parked our bikes near a big trailer, and picked our way through the piles of rubble and around the heavy machinery that littered the lot the trailer sat on. "Nothing suspicious so far," said Shannon, peering around at the scene.

"This trailer must be the main office," said Stacey. We went up the steps, peered through the screen door, and saw a man sitting behind an incredibly messy desk. It was covered with papers in foot-high stacks, cardboard coffee cups, and empty doughnut boxes. The guy behind the desk was gesturing as he shouted into the phone. "No, not tomorrow," he yelled. "I need it today! And if it's not here by three — " He listened for a moment and then slammed the phone down. "Bums," he said, shaking his head. Then he looked up and saw us peeking through the door. He smiled. "Come on in," he said, waving us in.

We walked in, edging our way around file cabinets and piles of tools. "How can I help you girls?" he asked. "Here to rent a bulldozer?" He laughed.

"Um, no," I said. "Not exactly." I was trying to figure out how to ask him about the glass without raising his suspicions, when the phone rang.

He brushed aside a pile of papers and answered it, "Rockaway!" he barked. He listened for a moment. "No, no, no," he said. "That was *two* backhoes and *one* crane — "

We heard another phone ringing. "Hold on," he said, "I've got another call." He brushed some more papers aside and jabbed a button. "Hello?" he said. "Rockaway speaking." He listened again. "I told you before," he said, "It's a three-man crew, and they're working as fast as they can. Hold on a minute, will you? I need to finish up this other call." He jabbed at a button again. "Hello?" he said. "Hello?" He rolled his eyes and grinned at us.

"Lost them," he said. "Happens all the time. My secretary's the only one who knows how to work these darn phones." He pushed another button and found the call he'd put on hold. "Now, who is this again?" he asked.

Just then, two men wearing tool belts and Rockaway and Sons baseball caps walked into the office. The man on the phone turned to them, knocking over a half-filled cup as he did. The coffee ran all over a pile of papers, and started to drip down the side of his desk, but he didn't seem to notice. "Pete! Dave!" he said. "Just the men I was looking for." Then he spoke into the phone again. "Hold on one more second, okay?" He pushed a button, laid down the receiver, and started talking to the two men about a foundation that needed work. "I've got the work order right here," he said, shuffling through a stack of pink forms. He scratched his head. "At least, I *thought* it was here."

By this time, Shannon, Stacey, Claud, and I were just standing there with our mouths open. I, for one, could not believe how incredibly disorganized the office was. I raised my eyebrows at Claudia and shrugged. She shrugged, too. "Let's go," she whispered. "We're not going to get anywhere with this guy."

We headed for the door, and the man behind the desk smiled and waved. " 'Bye, girls," he said. "Sorry to keep you waiting. Come back some other time, when I'm not so busy."

We piled out of the trailer, and as soon as we were clear of the office we collapsed into giggles. "Some *other* time?" gasped Claudia.

"When he's not so *busy*?" I said.

"Like *when*?" asked Shannon.

Stacey just laughed until she could hardly breathe.

"I have *never* seen anybody so disorganized," I said.

"And so clumsy," Shannon added. "How can he possible run a successful business?"

"I don't get it," I said. "But obviously he'd never remember if he *did* supply that glass, and even if a miracle happened and he could, he'd never be able to find the purchase order. This was a definite dead end."

"Sorry, guys," said Claudia, looking sheepish. "I guess deductive reasoning doesn't always pay off."

"That's okay, it's not your fault. But I vote that we head for the set," said Stacey. "I mean, we should at least check up on Derek, don't you think?"

We hopped on our bikes and rode over to the set. It was a beautiful day, with white puffy clouds sailing through a perfect blue sky, but

I wasn't paying much attention to the scenery as I rode. Instead, I was thinking hard, trying to figure out what to do next. None of our detective work had paid off so far. Maybe it was time for more drastic measures.

I went over our list of suspects. Sheila Mayberry? I couldn't really imagine her causing the accidents, even though she was sure getting a lot of mileage out of them. Zeke Hill? I just saw him as a guy who was out of a job and desperate to be hired back. Frank Bottoms was a definite possibility: he *looked* like a villain, since he always wore black and loved to puff on those huge cigars. But somehow my gut instinct was to take a closer look at Carson Fraser. At first, I had thought he wasn't smart enough to pull off all those accidents. But a lot of things pointed in his direction: I could tell he couldn't stand Derek, since he didn't bother to hide it. He was always nearby when accidents happened. And he probably figured his star status would protect him if he was ever found out.

"Carson," I said out loud, as I rode along. "He's the one to watch." If I could only figure out a way to learn more about him. I worked on the problem during that whole bike ride, but no great ideas came to mind. Carson wasn't exactly the most approachable guy on the set. If he was nicer, my job would be easy:

I'd just try to strike up a conversation with him. But instead, he was a creep, and I was going to have to think of another way to find out more about him.

When we finally arrived at the set, I led my friends over to the actors' lounge, where Derek and Todd were sitting with their parents. Frank Bottoms was there, but I didn't see Carson.

It felt strange to be on the set without any official reason. "How's it going?" I asked Derek.

"Don't ask," he said. He shot a quick glance at Frank, who appeared to be napping in his chair with the ever-present cigar still in his mouth. "Carson's been flubbing his lines all morning," Derek whispered. "I don't think he even *read* this part of the script before today. Harry told the rest of us to take a break, and he pulled Carson into his trailer for 'a little talk.' "

"Oh, really?" I asked. That was interesting. Carson was in Harry's trailer. And Frank Bottoms was napping in his chair. That meant that *Carson's* trailer would be empty. Suddenly, I had a great idea.

I pulled my friends off to one side. "Listen," I hissed. "I'm going to go snoop around in

Carson's trailer. I just *know* I'll find some evidence there."

"Kristy!" said Stacey, looking shocked. "Are you out of your mind?"

"You can't do *that*!" Claudia added.

"It's too dangerous," put in Shannon.

"I guess that means none of you are coming with me," I said. "That's okay. Just keep a lookout for me, will you? I don't want to get caught in there. Give a whistle or something if you see Carson coming." I took off toward Carson's trailer without waiting to hear any more arguments about my plan.

As I approached the door with Carson's name next to it, I looked around to make sure nobody was watching. Then I took a deep breath, eased open the door and slipped through it.

The inside of the trailer was dim, since the mini-blinds were down, but as soon as my eyes adjusted I could see just fine. Now, I have to say that I don't advocate snooping around, but just this once I let my curiosity get the better of me, After all, there was a chance I'd find something important. Here's what I learned about Carson: His favorite snack food appears to be those little miniature Ritz-cracker-and-peanut-butter sandwiches — there were several opened boxes lying around. He is even more in love with himself than I had guessed, judging by the number of mirrors in the place. He has a friend in Missouri named Neil, to whom he sends boring postcards: there was a half-written one on the coffee table. And he must be flattered by the attention he gets from that girl who always wears a rose in her button-hole. I knew *that* because there was a whole bowl full of roses, ranging from fresh to very, very wilted, which he had saved. She must give him the rose she wears every day. Next to the bowl was the freshest rose of the batch, and next to *that* was a pile of notes. The one on top said, "From your favorite fan, you-know-who." It had X's and O's and little hearts drawn all over it, and a lipstick kiss near the word "fan."

But nothing I'd seen made me suspicious. There wasn't a single, solitary clue to prove that Carson was out to get Derek. I had just started to poke around in a tiny, overstuffed closet when I heard a strange hissing noise. I stopped to listen, and realized somebody was whispering my name. I ran to the window, peeked through the blinds, and saw Shannon. Her face was bright red, and she looked aw-fully anxious. "Kristy!" she hissed, louder this time.

I went to the door and opened it a crack. "What's up?" I asked.

"Kristy! Get out of there, fast!" she said, looking as if she were about to pass out. "Carson just came out of Harry's trailer, and he's heading this way!"

I jumped down from the trailer, closed the door behind me, and ran off with Shannon. When we met up with Stacey and Claudia, the relief on their faces was obvious. "Do me a favor, Kristy," said Claudia. "Don't ever, *ever* do anything like that again!"

I crossed my fingers behind my back and promised. Even though the only thing my visit to Carson's trailer had produced was some very nervous friends, I knew I would do it again if it would keep Derek safe.

CHAPTER 12

Thursday

Congratulations, Mal! We're all so proud of you. First, to be picked out of the crowd like that, and then to do such a terrific job — it was awesome. And to think I almost missed your performance. If it wasn't for Kristy, I might have. Her brilliant idea saved the day.

Brilliant — that's me. Not that I like to boast about it or anything, but I do have to admit that Mary Anne's entry in the club notebook was right on. But maybe I'd better back up and explain everything.

First of all, what Mary Anne was congratulating Mal for was this: the day before, Mal had finally made it over to the set. Since it was late in the afternoon, she was through sitting for Claire, and she had come to watch the filming for awhile. She was hanging out on the sidelines with me and Claud, watching Derek film a scene. Right in the middle of one of his lines, I felt a sneeze coming on. I tried to stop it — I really did! — but it popped out. It was a loud one, too.

"Cut!" said Harry disgustedly. Everybody on the set turned to stare at me, including Harry himself.

"Sorry!" I squeaked.

But then I realized Harry wasn't looking at me anymore. He was looking at Mal, and he was smiling. "Hey, you," he said. "Red! Ever acted before?"

"Me?" asked Mal. She had suddenly turned white.

"Yes, *you*. You with the glasses and freckles and that great hair. You'd be perfect for this walk-on I have planned for tomorrow. You wouldn't have any lines, understand. And you'd only be on the screen for about a half-second — "

"I'll do it!" said Mal, grinning.

Later, as we walked home, Mal was beside herself. "I can't believe it!" she said. "He liked my looks. He *liked* my looks!" She reminded us of the time we were all in California, and she and Jessi were visiting Derek on the set of his TV show. Earlier, Jessi had gotten a part as an extra, and that day the director was asking for extras again. When Mal volunteered, he gave her a glance and said her looks were wrong. She was *crushed*, especially because she'd been going through this make-over phase — dyeing her hair blonde and wearing makeup — and *she* thought she looked great.

Anyway, Mal's California experience only made it that much better when Harry picked her out of a crowd based on her own, true looks. We were all thrilled for her, and Mary Anne volunteered to take care of Vanessa and Margo and Claire the next morning so Mal could get to the set early.

So Mary Anne was sitting for Mal's three little sisters. And the second she arrived that morning, Vanessa and Margo started in on her. "We *have* to go to the set," said Vanessa. "Mal's going to be a star!"

"We *promised* her we'd come and watch," said Margo.

"I'd love to see her, too," said Mary Anne, glancing at Claire, who hadn't said a word yet. "How about it, Claire?"

"Uh-uh," said Claire, folding her arms over her chest. "I'm not going."

"Don't you want to see Mal make a movie?" asked Mary Anne. "That's not something that happens every day, you know."

"I don't care," said Claire, pouting. But Mary Anne thought she saw a glimmer of interest in Claire's eyes.

"Come on, Claire," begged Margo. "If you won't go, *we* can't go. Don't be a scaredy cat."

"I'm *not* a scaredy cat," said Claire with dignity. "Everyone's afraid of vampires."

"But vampires aren't real!" said Vanessa.

"They are to me," said Claire.

Mary Anne sighed. "We could have ice cream on the way home," she said, hating herself for trying to bribe Claire.

Claire stood her ground. "We had ice cream last night," she said.

At this point, Margo lost it. "It's not *fair*!" she yelled. "Just because Claire's a big chicken, she has to spoil everything." She stomped off to her room, and Vanessa followed her.

"It's not my fault I'm scared," said Claire,

when she and Mary Anne were alone. "I can't help it." She looked upset.

"I know," said Mary Anne. She gave Claire a big hug. "Why don't you look at your book for awhile?" she said, settling Claire on the couch. Then she headed for the phone and dialed my number. As Mary Anne knew, I was home that morning because once again both Mr. and Mrs. Masters were planning to be on the set all day. I was still going to go over there, just to watch Mal do her scene, but for the moment I was enjoying a morning off.

"Kristy," said Mary Anne, when I answered the phone. "You have to help me."

"What's up?" I asked, gulping down the last bite of my pancake.

"It's Claire," said Mary Anne. "She refuses to go to the set, and Margo and Vanessa really want to watch Mal. So do I, for that matter."

I felt bad. I'd sworn to solve Claire's vampire problem, but I hadn't done a thing about it. It was now or never. I thought hard, but my mind was a blank.

"I know vampires are scary," Mary Anne was saying, "but after all, there *are* scarier things in the world. Why on earth did Claire have to pick vampires?"

"That's it!" I said.

"*What's* it?" asked Mary Anne.

"There are scarier things than vampires," I said, excitedly. "Suppose Claire were to dress up as the scariest thing she could think of. Maybe you could convince her that if she looked scary enough, the vampires would be afraid of *her*."

Mary Anne was silent for a second. "Kristy," she said, finally. "You're amazing. I think you've done it again. I'll give it a try, and maybe we'll see you at the set!"

When she'd hung up, Mary Anne went to find Claire. "Claire, let me ask you something," she said. "What's the scariest thing you can think of — *besides* vampires?"

"Witches," said Claire, promptly. "But they're only scary for *some* people. *I'm* not afraid of them. I was a witch last Halloween, and everybody was scared of me. Even Nicky."

"Perfect!" said Mary Anne, under her breath.

"What?" asked Claire.

"Nothing," said Mary Anne. "It's just that I was thinking . . ."

"Thinking *what*?" asked Claire.

"What if you got out your costume and put it on?" asked Mary Anne. "If witches are that scary, maybe even vampires would be afraid of you. You could wear your costume to the set, and you'd be perfectly safe." She crossed her fingers and hoped for the best.

Claire thought it over — for a total of about two seconds. Like most kids, she *loves* to dress up. All she needs is an excuse, and Mary Anne had just given her a great one.

"Stay right here and don't move," she told Mary Anne. "I'll be right back." She dashed upstairs.

Mary Anne waited patiently, and about ten minutes later she was well rewarded. When Claire came back down, she was completely transformed. She was wearing a long black gown that trailed on the floor, a black wig that was almost as long as the gown, and a pointy black hat. "Boo!" said Claire proudly, making a scary face and holding out her fingers like claws.

"Woo!" said Mary Anne, admiring the effect. "You sure do look scary. Tell me, are you a *real* witch?"

Claire giggled. "No, but don't tell anybody, okay?"

"I won't," said Mary Anne. "I especially won't tell any vampires. Ready to head for the set?"

Claire paused. "Are you *sure* I really look scary?" she asked.

"I'm positive," said Mary Anne.

Fifteen minutes later, Mary Anne and Claire

were on the set, along with Margo and Vanessa. "Mal!" yelled Margo, spotting her sister emerging from the makeup trailer. "We're here! We're here!"

Mal waved, looking a little bewildered when she saw Claire.

"No more yelling," Mary Anne told Margo. "We have to be really, really quiet if we're going to stay and watch." Mary Anne looked up just then and spotted me. We gave each other the thumbs-up sign, and I headed over to join them. Then, all of a sudden, I noticed Mary Anne looking at something behind me. Her eyes had gotten very, very wide. I turned to find out what she was looking at, and almost jumped out of my skin. Following me was a vampire in full costume and makeup, and he was heading *straight* for Claire. Her back was to him, so she hadn't spotted him yet, but he was approaching fast. Mary Anne and I exchanged looks. There wasn't a thing we could do but cross our fingers and hold our breath.

"Hey, little witch!" said the vampire to Claire. She turned and saw him, and for a second I thought she was going to scream or cry. Then she drew herself up as tall as she could, gave a great cackling laugh, held out her "claws," and said, "Vampire, vampire, go away, *don't* come back some other day!" I guess that was her idea of a spell.

The vampire held up his hands. "Whoa!" he said. "*Please* don't hurt me, Miss Witch! I'll go away, I promise!" He backed away, winking at Mary Anne as he left.

"It worked!" yelled a jubilant Claire. "I scared him off! Silly old vampire. He didn't even know I wasn't a real witch."

"Thank goodness," Mary Anne whispered to me. "Your idea really saved the day."

"I couldn't have thought of it without you," I said modestly. But just like Claire, I was feeling pretty proud of myself. By that time, Claud, Stacey, and Shannon had shown up, and we all settled in with Mary Anne and the girls to watch Mal do her walk-on. She had to repeat it about three million times before Harry was satisfied. It wasn't Mal's fault that there were so many takes, though. It was Carson's. He couldn't seem to get his lines straight, as usual.

At the end of the day, an exhausted Mal walked home with her sisters and Mary Anne. Claire had her gown tucked up so it wouldn't drag, and she practiced her cackling as she walked.

"Well, I've decided something," said Mal. "I'm pretty sure I don't want to be a movie star. It's hard work! And it's not that exciting, really."

"I decided something, too," announced Claire. "Vampires are nothing but big scaredy cats!" She grinned and let out one last cackle, and Mal and Mary Anne smiled at each other. Claire's vampire-phobia was a thing of the past.

CHAPTER 13

"Could I have everybody's attention please?" It was a hot Monday morning, and Cliff Chase stood in the middle of the set, holding up his hands. "People?" The buzz of activity slowly came to a halt, and a circle of actors, gaffers, grips, cameramen, and makeup people formed around the director.

"I just wanted to say that I'm very happy with the way filming has been going. You've all been working hard, and it's paid off. We have one more week here on location, and then we'll head back to the Coast to finish up some of the interior shots on the lot." He paused. "We have plenty to do this week, but if we stay focused we can do it. That's it!" He smiled. The crowd broke up and Derek and I looked at each other.

"One more week!" I said. "Just when I was getting used to this schedule. It's really been fun, Derek."

"I know," he said. "It's been great to be back in Stoneybrook. Even though I've been working, it's almost like summer vacation. I don't even have to have a tutor on the set, the way I do when we're filming *P.S. 162*. Instead, I can just hang out with you, which is a lot more fun."

I gave him a little hug. I was so relieved that he hadn't had any more major accidents. In fact, I was almost beginning to wonder whether the whole mystery was just in my mind. Was somebody *really* out to get Derek, or were the accidents all just coincidence? Then I remembered the nasty note, and I shivered. My main job, I knew, was to make sure Derek made it through the rest of that week unharmed.

Derek was only shooting one more scene that day: he'd be leaving at noon to meet his parents and go to an appointment in New York City. His driver, Mr. Mead, was standing by to take him there, and while Derek was in makeup, Mr. Mead and I talked for awhile. He was an interesting guy, and I could tell he thought the world of Derek. "He's a smart kid," Mr. Mead said. "Polite, too. Not like some of the other folks I have to drive around."

I felt proud of Derek. "I know," I said. "I'll really miss him when he goes back to California."

"He'll miss you, too," said Mr. Mead. "He talks about you all the time. It's 'Kristy this and Kristy that' every morning."

I beamed. Just then, I spotted Claud making her way toward us. "Hi!" I called. "What are *you* doing here? Todd's not filming today."

"I know," she said. "I just felt like hanging out. Missy said she'd let me watch her do Carson's vampire makeup later today." She smiled at Mr. Mead and said hello.

"Well, girls, I'm going to head for Derek's trailer," said Mr. Mead. "He invited me to use it today while I'm waiting, and I've got an important nap planned."

After Mr. Mead left, Claud and I strolled around the set, watching the gaffers and cameramen set up for the day's filming. "Hey, where's Cokie these days?" Claud asked me.

"I don't know," I said. "I haven't seen her since the party. Maybe she was embarrassed about everybody getting sick. Or maybe she really *did* poison us on purpose, and now she's lying low, trying to avoid suspicion. In any case, I'm glad she's been staying away from the set. That gives me one less suspect to watch out for."

"Our detective work hasn't paid off yet, has it?" Claud said, frowning. "And we only have one more week. After that, Derek will be back in California, where we can't keep an eye on him."

That really made me think. I realized that my job wasn't *only* to protect Derek while he was here in Stoneybrook. If I didn't solve the mystery soon, Derek might be in just as much jeopardy back in California. "Claudia, this is serious," I said. "We need to figure out who's after Derek before it's too late. I feel like I have to *do* something — right *now*. Since you're here, maybe you could look out for Derek while I investigate. He's probably almost finished in makeup. Would you stay with him for awhile when he's done?"

"Sure," said Claud. "No problem. Just be careful, okay?"

"I will," I said. I left Claud sitting in the actors' lounge and started to wander around the set, looking for suspects. I knew Carson was in makeup, and for a moment I thought about going back into his trailer to poke around some more. I walked over to check it out. The window shades were up, and I peered inside, then stepped back quickly. Frank Bottoms was sitting on a chair near the window, leafing through a magazine. So much for *that* plan.

As I stood near Carson's trailer, trying to figure out what to do next, I noticed Sheila

Mayberry walking by, talking with a red-haired woman and a blonde girl. I fell into step behind them, trying to overhear the conversation. At first, I couldn't tell what they were talking about. Sheila, in a peach-colored suit, seemed to be rattling on enthusiastically about something. I walked a little faster, trying to close the distance between us.

"I just *know* *Variety*'s audience will want to read about what's going on here," Sheila was saying to the red-haired woman. She lowered her voice, but I could still hear what she said next. "Some people are actually saying there might be a *curse* on this set, you know," she added.

The red-haired woman, whom I now assumed was a reporter for *Variety*, took some notes. "And what's *your* role here?" she asked the blonde girl.

"Oh, I just try to help out wherever I can," said the girl. "My name's Lindsey Rockaway — that's R-O-C-K-A-W-A-Y — and I'm a *huge* fan of Carson Fraser's. His biggest fan ever, probably. I was just telling Sheila about the fan club I want to start, and she was giving me some tips . . ."

Lindsey went on, but I had stopped listening. Right after she had told the reporter her name, she had turned to wave at somebody, and I had noticed the red rose in her button-hole.

That's when I started to put a few things together.

First of all, her name was Lindsey Rocka-way. It took me a second to remember why that name was familiar, and then I had a sud-den image of the busy man in the trailer of-fice. Could she be one of *those* Rockaways? If she was, that might mean she had access to some of the materials they delivered. And then there were those red roses in her buttonhole . . . and heaped up in Carson's trailer. This girl, I realized, had been on the set every single day. Maybe I had another suspect on my hands.

"Well, 'bye," I heard Lindsey say. "I have some errands to do. Nice to meet you!" She shook hands with the reporter, smiled at Sheila, and walked away. In a split second, I made a big decision. I would follow her for awhile, just to see if I could learn a little more about her.

She started to walk fast, dodging grips pushing hand carts, and wardrobe people with loads of costumes. Then she was heading off the set, toward the street where all the cars were parked.

Just as she stepped off the curb, I heard

somebody call my name. I turned to see Charlie waving to me. He was standing next to a huge light, holding it up while one of the gaffers adjusted it.

"Kristy!" he yelled. "Come here for a second."

"I'm busy!" I called back.

"This'll just take a second," he said.

Reluctantly, I went over to talk to him. "What's up?" I asked.

He told me that he was planning to stay late that day, and that I'd have to find my own way home. "I'm sure Watson will come and pick you up if you call him," he said. "I'm really sorry, Kristy."

"No problem," I said distractedly. "I have a BSC meeting later today, anyway. I'll just walk over to Claud's. Is that it?"

"That's it," he said, giving me a quizzical look. "Hey, are you okay, Kristy? You seem tense."

"I'm fine," I said. "But I have to run. See you!" I took off toward the spot where I'd last seen Lindsey, but she was nowhere in sight. "Lost her!" I said, smacking my fist into my palm. I spent the next half hour roaming the set, trying to spot that stringy blonde hair and the red rose, but I didn't see her anywhere. Suddenly, it seemed incredibly important to find her. Now that I thought about it, there

124

was definitely something suspicious about the way she hung around the set. And I knew that any fan of Carson's had the potential to be an enemy of Derek's.

Just as I was about to give up on finding her and start looking for Claud and Derek instead, she popped into view. She had come from behind one of the big trailers, and she looked *awful*. Her hair was all messed up, the rose had disappeared, and her fingers were black with what looked like mud. For a second, I wondered what she had been up to, but then she started walking and I had to concentrate on following her. No way did I want to lose her again!

She left the set and began walking quickly toward downtown Stoneybrook. I followed close behind her, dodging behind bushes and trees every now and then so I wouldn't be noticed.

We walked all the way downtown, which took almost fifteen minutes. I glanced at my watch and noticed that it was nearly noon. I wanted to be back on the set before Derek left, which didn't leave much time. But I decided to stay with Lindsey, at least until I found out where she was heading.

Finally, she pulled open the door of a convenience store. I paused outside, and then decided to follow her in. She went straight to the refrigerator case, pulled out a can of soda, and headed back to the cash register. I ducked behind the magazine stand and kept watching.

She reached into her backpack and rummaged around. I figured she was looking for her wallet, and I was right. When she pulled it out, something fell out of the backpack and landed behind her on the floor. She didn't seem to notice. She just paid for her soda and left the store. I jumped out from behind the magazines, picked up what she had dropped, and ran out the door behind her.

Lindsey didn't seem to be in a hurry anymore, once she had left the store. She plopped herself on a bench, opened the soda, and took a gulp. As soon as I saw that she was settled, I ducked around the corner to take a better look at what I had picked up.

It was a book — a car repair manual, all greasy and worn. At first, I was disappointed. I had been hoping for some evidence. Then I started to leaf through it, and what I found made my heart start racing like mad.

The corner of page 137 was turned down, as if to mark something important. And page 137 was all about brakes. *Brake malfunctions*, read the chapter heading. I scanned the paragraphs below it, and saw that somebody had used yellow highlighter to emphasize three sentences. And those sentences explained the main causes of brake failure.

"Oh, no!" I said out loud, thinking of Lindsey's blackened hands and messy hair. That wasn't mud on her hands — it was grease! She had been fooling around under a car. And if the car she had been fooling around with was the one Mr. Mead drove . . . I gasped. "Derek!" I breathed. Then I started to run as fast as I could.

CHAPTER 14

"Gotta run," I panted. "Gotta make it. Keep moving, keep moving." I talked to myself as I ran. People stared at me as I zoomed by, and I knew they thought I was nuts, but I didn't care. I had only one thing on my mind.

The day had started out hot, and by that time, at high noon, it was sweltering. Sweat was pouring off me, and it was hard to breathe, but I just kept on running, clutching the book Lindsey had dropped. In my mind, I could picture Mr. Mead sliding behind the wheel of the car. Derek would be settled in the back seat, leaning against the cool cushions and enjoying the feel of the air-conditioning. He might even be closing his eyes for a short nap. Mr. Mead would put the car into gear and pull out of his parking space. Then he'd head down the road, never knowing that his brakes might not be working. What if a car pulled out in front of them? What if Mr. Mead went flying through a red light at a big intersection? "Gotta run," I told myself again, panting. "Save Derek."

Finally, I saw parked trucks up ahead. I put on one last burst of speed and sprinted through the set toward them, hoping I'd spot Derek's car before he drove away. I scanned the lines of parked cars, trucks, and vans, but the black sedan was nowhere in sight. "Oh, no," I moaned. "They already left!"

I slowed to a walk. If Mr. Mead had already pulled out, there was nothing I could do. Anyway, maybe I *was* nuts. Maybe there was nothing wrong with the car. Maybe there was some other, perfectly good explanation for the mess on Lindsey's hands.

I was just starting to think about what to do next when I walked around a van and spotted Mr. Mead climbing into the front seat of the black car and slamming the door. "Mr. Mead!" I yelled, starting to run again. "Derek!"

I was close enough so that I could see Mr. Mead putting on his seat belt. In a second, he'd start the car and drive away. "No, no!" I shouted. "Wait!" But the windows were all rolled up because of the air-conditioning. I heard the engine start. I had reached the car by then, and I began to bang on Mr. Mead's window. "Stop!" I said. Mr. Mead looked up, startled. I glanced into the back seat and saw Derek staring at me.

Mr. Mead rolled down the window. "What is it, Kristy?" he asked. "Are you coming with us?"

"No," I said. "Mr. Mead, please turn the car off!"

He looked at me questioningly, but he did as I asked. "What is it, Kristy?" he repeated.

"I think something may be wrong with the car," I said. "I think the brakes may not be working."

Mr. Mead was obviously a man who took things seriously. He didn't laugh at me, or ask any more questions. Instead, he got out of the car and bent down to look beneath it. Derek got out, too. "What's up, Kristy?" asked Derek.

"I'm not sure," I said. "Let's wait and see what Mr. Mead finds."

Mr. Mead was staring at a puddle of liquid near one of the rear tires. "That's brake fluid, if I'm not mistaken," he said. He bent further to check behind the wheel. "*Smells* like brake fluid," he said.

By that time, a crowd of movie people had gathered. They must have followed me when I ran through the set looking terrified. I saw one of the gaffers that Charlie sometimes worked with, a couple of makeup people, and a bunch of grips and assistants. "What's going on?" asked one of the grips.

"Looks like the brake line might have been cut," said Mr. Mead, standing up and dusting off his hands.

"Whoa!" said Derek. "That means the brakes wouldn't have worked at all, right?" He gulped.

"Right," said Mr. Mead. He gave me a curious look. "And Kristy was the one who stopped us in time," he continued.

A murmur ran through the crowd. "How'd *you* know about it?" asked the gaffer.

Suddenly I felt on the spot. I couldn't tell whether Mr. Mead and the people watching thought I was a heroine or a potential murderer. "I didn't do it!" I said. "It was — " I stopped, trying to figure out how to explain. I held up the car repair manual. "I saw somebody drop this," I began. Then, at the edge of the crowd, I spied Lindsey. I couldn't believe my eyes. She was strolling along casually, still sipping from that same can of soda. Her stringy hair was back in place, and her hands were a little cleaner. She looked like any other girl on the set — but I knew better. She was dangerous. And she must have come back to the set just so she could watch Derek's car drive off. I realized that she must be a very sick person.

"It was her!" I said, pointing at Lindsey. I didn't *mean* to make a big dramatic moment out of it, but it turned into one. Everybody whipped around to stare at Lindsey, and I saw her face turn white. "She's the one who did it," I added.

Lindsey narrowed her eyes. "What are you talking about?" she asked, smoothing her hair. "I didn't do anything. I've been downtown." She started to walk away, but the crowd closed in around her, as if by instinct.

"Somebody call the police!" I said. "This girl cut those brake lines, and I can prove it." My voice was a little shaky, and I guess Derek noticed because he came to stand next to me and slipped his hand into mine. Lindsey was staring at me angrily, and I stared right back at her. "Look at her hands," I said. "See all that grease under her fingernails? It's there because she was fooling around under this car." I smacked the top of Derek's sedan.

The crowd turned back and forth, watching first me and then Lindsey. They looked like spectators at a tennis match. For a second, I wanted to laugh, but I think it was just out of nervousness.

"You're crazy," said Lindsey. "I wouldn't

even know a brake line if I *saw* one."

My nervousness disappeared. "Oh *yeah*?" I said. I held the car repair manual up again. "Well, if you didn't know about brake lines before, you sure did after you read *this*!" I turned to Mr. Mead, and spoke loudly enough so that the crowd — and Lindsey — could hear me. "The police'll find her fingerprints all *over* this book, I'm sure of it." Suddenly, I realized that I might have made a big mistake. *My* fingerprints would be all over the book, too! But then Lindsey started to cry, and my mistake didn't matter anymore.

"It's all true," Lindsey sobbed. "She's right. I *did* cut the brake lines." She put her face in her hands. One of the grips eased an arm around her shoulders.

"Why?" asked Derek. "Why did you do it?"

"Because of Carson," said Lindsey, through her tears. "I love him."

"Carson?" asked Mr. Mead. "Isn't he one of those young actors?"

"He's not just any actor, he's the *best* actor," said Lindsey, sounding shrill. "The *best*. But you'd never know it, because *he*" — she sniffed, nodding at Derek — "kept stealing all the scenes."

Derek looked pale. I bet I did, too.

The crowd grew quiet as Lindsey rambled on and on about how unfair it was that Derek got more attention than Carson, and how she had finally figured out that the only way to help Carson was to "put Derek out of the picture." I think everybody, Derek included, could see what *I* had figured out just moments before: Lindsey was a very disturbed person.

"Major weirdness!"

"She's really sick!"

"I feel sorry for her."

Those were my friends talking, later that afternoon at our BSC meeting. I had filled them in on the story so far, and they were amazed at what had happened. None of us had suspected Lindsey, so it all came as a total surprise. Of course, that last comment was made by Mary Anne, who never judges anyone and always has sympathy for the underdog.

"So, let me make sure I have this right," said Stacey. "Because she felt so strongly about Carson, she tried to hurt Derek?"

"That's right," I said.

"But Derek's safe now," said Jessi. "Right?"

"Definitely," I said. "Lindsey's in police custody tonight, and I hear they'll probably be moving her someplace where she can be helped. Somewhere far, far away, I hope."

"I hope so, too," said Mal with a shiver. "What she did is pretty scary stuff."

As I had told my friends, Lindsey had confessed everything that afternoon. Although some of Derek's accidents *had* been caused by his clumsiness (dropping the lamp, for example), Lindsey had been responsible for setting up most of them. She had spilled oil on the floor the day he fell. She had switched the breakaway glass with *real* glass from her father's company. She had tampered with the harness used for the flying stunt. And she had, of course, been the one who sent the threatening note to Derek, the one I'd told Mrs. Masters about. Lucky thing I hadn't followed his agent's advice to quit worrying about it.

She'd sent some other notes, too, and I would have found them if I had poked around some more in Carson's trailer. After Lindsey was caught that afternoon, Carson had come forward with a stack of the notes she'd given him along with the roses. Some were mushy, like the one I'd seen. But some were scary. They had talked about how he didn't have to worry because she was going to "take care" of Derek. "I didn't take them *seriously*," a shaken Carson had told me. That was the first time I ever saw him drop his habitual cool act.

"There's just one more thing," said Claudia, popping the last bite of a Twizzler into her mouth as our meeting drew to a close. "What about Cokie's party?"

"Must have been just good old food poisoning," I said. "Lindsey wasn't even *at* the party, so it couldn't have been her fault."

"Either way, you'll never catch *me* eating Cokie's deviled eggs again," said Claud, holding her stomach and rolling her eyes.

We all cracked up. It was a relief to laugh. And it was an even *bigger* relief to know that Derek was safe. Like Mary Anne, I felt sorry for Lindsey — but I was glad she had been stopped before it was too late.

CHAPTER 15

A week later, it was all over. The cast and crew of *Little Vampires* had gone back to California, and of course Derek had gone with them. I missed him, and I missed being on the set every day, but I *didn't* miss worrying about him.

One really cool thing happened. The Masterses called Dawn when they got back to California, and asked her to do the same job there that I had done here. So, as filming finished up in L.A., Dawn was with Derek on the set almost every day. And as the summer went on, her letters kept us up-to-date on all the latest *Little Vampires* happenings.

Once the movie people left, life in Stoneybrook returned to normal. At first, I wondered if it would end up being a boring summer. After all, there was a lot *left* of the summer, and the movie shoot was a hard act to follow. But my worries were groundless. Just reading the newspapers and magazines gave me and my friends plenty of excitement and lots to talk about. There were articles about *Little Vampires* almost every day, and not just in the local paper, either. Thanks to Sheila Mayberry, *Little Vampires* — and the little town of Stoneybrook — had made the national news.

I started to collect all the clippings, plus Dawn's letters, for a scrapbook, and my friends pitched in to help. Between us, we put together quite a "memory book." In fact, maybe I should just let the scrapbook speak for itself, and you'll see what I mean.

Dear Kristy,

Well, you were right about life on the set of Little Vampires. It's never boring, that's for sure! Derek is still doing a terrific job, and he hasn't had even one tiny accident. Carson doesn't seem like such a bad guy. Maybe that experience with Lindsey taught him a lesson. Cliff Chase apologized publicly to Zeke and rehired him to finish the movie. And Sheila Mayberry is still as busy as ever, as I'm sure you know. It seems I can't read a newspaper or a magazine these days without seeing something about Little Vampires! Well, gotta go. I'm needed on the set.

Love, Dawn

P.S. I'm glad to hear that Claire's fear of vampires hasn't returned. I'll have to remember to try that "cure" next time the We ♥ Kids Club has a fearful client. It's a winner, Kristy!

From the Stoneybrook News (this article is my personal favorite!):

LOCAL GIRL SAVES ACTOR'S LIFE

Tragedy was averted yesterday when Stoneybrook resident Kristy Thomas stopped a limousine driver from starting up his car. On a tip from Ms. Thomas, the driver, John Mead, inspected the car's brake lines and found that they had been cut. Police say there was a good chance that

Mr. Mead and his passenger, actor Derek Masters, would have been injured had the car been driven. The police assume foul play, and a suspect has been taken into custody . . .

From the _Stoneybrook News_, two weeks later:

Stoneybrook police announced today that charges have been dropped against a local juvenile who was found to have cut the brake lines on a car leased by actor Derek Masters. "I don't want her to go to jail," the young actor was quoted as saying. "I just hope she gets some help." The juvenile is being treated at Hidden Acres, a private Massachusetts facility for emotionally disturbed adolescents.

What young blond teen idol has at least one fan who might have been just a little *too* devoted? Hint: Next time you see him, he'll be sporting fangs . . .

From *Variety*:

Despite early rumors of trouble on the set, the made-for-TV movie *Little Vampires* is getting terrific word-of-mouth around town. Filming is nearly completed, and a "Making of . . ." is slated to air later this month. The special will showcase one of the quaintest little towns on the Eastern Seaboard: Stoneybrook, Connecticut, where much of the filming was done . . .

From *People Weekly's* Insider column:

Our sources tell us that the made-for-TV movie *Little Vampires* is sure to be a big winner. Early on, it looked as if the movie might never wrap: some were even saying there was a curse on the film. Well, so much for superstition . . .

If you combine an affection for vampires with a liking for Norman Rockwell-type scenes of small-town life, and have any curiosity about behind-the-scenes action, be sure to catch next week's special, *The Making of Little Vampires*. The process of shooting this teen-star vehicle wasn't smooth, and this special doesn't pull any punches: It details all the mishaps that plagued the production during the early weeks of filming. But as we all know, there's a happy ending — the movie just finished shooting and the buzz says it's a sure hit . . .

From Top Teen Starz:

Girls are flipping over Derek Masters, one of the young stars of the upcoming made-for-TV movie *Little Vampires*. Derek says he's too young to date, but you can still dream! Check out our full-size pinup on page 52 . . .

From the Stoneybrook News:

The town of Stoneybrook will be featured in a TV special this Wednesday night. The special, *The Making of Little Vampires*, includes many scenes that will be familiar

142

to Stoneybrook residents. To see Stoneybrook Elementary as you've never seen it before, tune in on Wednesday at eight . . .

Dear Kristy,
  I saw you on TV last night! Did you see yourself? It was in that one scene at the school, where Carson was arguing with Harry. You were standing right behind Derek, wearing a red T-shirt. I nearly jumped out of my seat when I saw you...
    Love, Dawn

From *Top Teen Starz*:

Win a date with Carson Fraser, the hunkiest vampire this side of Transylvania. Just tell us, in 50 words or less, why *you'd* like to be Carson's next victim . . .

Fang Alert! Get out your garlic and your wooden stakes, and get ready for a rollicking good time (plus a few truly touching moments) in the biggest hit of the fall season. Little Vampires is coming your way . . .

Dear Kristy,

It's a wrap! That, as you know, is movie language for "it's all finished." Filming ended yesterday. I'm going to miss being on the set every day, but I'll tell you one thing I won't miss: Carson Fraser! He's developed such a big head from all those articles in the teen magazines. Derek is in them all the time, too, but you don't catch him preening in every mirror he passes. (Good thing Carson isn't a real vampire. If he was, he *wouldn't be able to see his precious reflection!)*

WBS!

Love, Dawn

Well, that's my scrapbook — so far. I'm saving the last few pages for the reviews of *Little Vampires*, which I can hardly wait to see. Dawn called Mary Anne last night and told her that Derek's parents are trying to set up a special preview for Stoneybrook residents, which would be totally cool. But if that doesn't work out, I'll see it this fall, when it's on TV. Meanwhile, I plan to relax and enjoy what's left of this Interesting Summer!

About the Author

ANN M. MARTIN did *a lot* of baby-sitting when she was growing up in Princeton, New Jersey. She is a former editor of books for children, and was graduated from Smith College.

Ms. Martin lives in New York City with her cats, Mouse and Rosie. She likes ice cream and *I Love Lucy*; and she hates to cook.

Ann Martin's Apple Paperbacks include *Yours Turly, Shirley; Ten Kids, No Pets; With You and Without You; Bummer Summer*; and all the other books in the Baby-sitters Club series.

Look for Mystery #16

CLAUDIA AND THE CLUE
IN THE PHOTOGRAPH

I turned up the volume, and we all listened.
"A recent surprise audit has uncovered a
major deficit in the bank's holdings," the reporter said, sounding very serious. I wasn't
exactly sure what she meant by that, but as
she kept talking, it became pretty clear. There
was a *ton* of money missing from the bank —
and no way to explain why.

The reporter went on to say that the police
had already ruled out the possibility of "trans-
action error" (Stacey said that meant, like, if
a clerk had put ten too many zeros after a
number of something), and that the bank's
video cameras showed no signs of a robbery
or forcible entry. Then she said that the bank
was asking for anybody with information or
tips to call a special number. Then the bulletin
ended, and Billy Blue came back on, in the
middle of singing "I'm Lost Without You."

"That was big news," I said. "I mean that could be *our* money that's missing."

"Do you have an account at that bank?" asked Shannon.

"Well, no," I admitted. "But I *might* have opened one, if I ever decided to save my money. Anyway, I was just thinking — wouldn't it be wild if there was a clue to the crime in one of those pictures I took on Sunday? I mean, I must have shot a zillion pictures of that bank."

"Oh, Claud, you've been watching too many late-night movies," said Stacey.

"There *is* a movie about something like that happening," Mary Anne said thoughtfully. "I can't think of the title, but it's about this photographer who takes a picture of a murder — by mistake, I mean. He only finds out about it later, when he develops the pictures."

"See?" I said. "It could happen."

"Sure it could," said Kristy. "But it doesn't seem too likely. I mean, we don't even know when the crime took place. It'd be a major coincidence if it happened last Sunday."

"Kristy's right," said Stacey. " I mean, this isn't *Nancy Drew and the Mystery of the Bank.*"

"I don't care what you all say. I'm going to develop that film — tonight," I said.

Read all the latest books
in the Baby-sitters Club series
by Ann M. Martin

Mysteries:

Don't miss out on
The All New

BABY·SITTERS®

Fan Club

Join now!
Your one-year membership package includes:

- The exclusive Fan Club T-Shirt!
- A Baby-sitters Club poster!
- A Baby-sitters Club note pad and pencil!
- An official membership card!
- The exclusive *Guide to Stoneybrook!*

Plus four additional newsletters per year

so you can be the first to know the hot news about the series — Super Specials, Mysteries, Videos, and more — the baby-sitters, Ann Martin, and lots of baby-sitting fun from the Baby-sitters Club Headquarters!

ALL THIS FOR JUST $6.95 plus $1.00 postage and handling! **You can't get all this great stuff anywhere else except THE BABY-SITTERS FAN CLUB!**

Just fill in the coupon below and mail with payment to: THE BABY-SITTERS FAN CLUB, Scholastic Inc., P.O. Box 7500, 2931 E. McCarty Street, Jefferson City, MO 65102.

THE BABY-SITTERS FAN CLUB

___ YES! Enroll me in The Baby-sitters Fan Club! I've enclosed my check or money order (no cash please) for $7.95

Name _____ Birthdate _____

Street _____

City _____ State/Zip _____

Where did you buy this book?

- ❏ Bookstore
- ❏ Book Fair
- ❏ Drugstore
- ❏ Book Club
- ❏ Supermarket
- ❏ other_____

BSFC593

Now THE BABY-SITTERS CLUB

is a Video Club too!